The Plague of Hollywood

Derek Rushlow

Copyright © 2024 by Derek Rushlow

All rights reserved.

No part of this publication may be reproduced, distributed, or transmitted in any form or by any means, including photocopying, recording, or other electronic or mechanical methods, without the prior written permission of the publisher, except in the case of brief quotations embodied in critical reviews and certain other noncommercial uses permitted by copyright law.

Any references to historical events, real people, or real places are used fictitiously. Names, characters, and places are products of the author's imagination.

For inquiries regarding rights, permissions, or other business matters, please contact: derekrushlow81@gmail.com

ISBN: 9798339894520

Cover design by Rebeccacovers

Also by Derek Rushlow

Night of the Clowns
Who's Charlie?

Introduction

The red carpet.

No, not the one celebrities walk on at special events. The one in my kindergarten class.

One day, as we sat with our little hands folded in our little laps, our teacher asked us what we wanted to be when we grew up. Some of my classmates said police officer, firefighter, or astronaut. A few of the girls said they wanted to be princesses. They elaborated by saying they would live in castles and have golden crowns.

When it was my turn, I said I wanted to be a zookeeper. My parents had taken my brother and me to the San Diego Zoo, and while there, we watched as one of the zookeepers fed the flamingos.

I grew up in California, surrounded by sunny days and trips to places like the zoo. Meanwhile, across the country, Ethan Mitchell was a kid growing up in Minnesota, where winters were long and harsh, but his imagination stayed warm. He didn't know it then, but his passion for filmmaking would one day take him far beyond the cold of Minnesota.

"What is he doing?" I asked my parents.

Since my dad was too busy trying to control my restless brother, Adam, my mom replied, "He's feeding the flamingos."

Even as a small child, I knew I had to be more straightforward. "Why is he in there?"

"He has to feed them," she answered.

I sighed, a little frustrated that she wasn't answering my question to my satisfaction—something that was utterly no fault of her own. "Why is he with them, and we can't be?" I asked, thinking the third time would be the charm.

Finally, she gave me the answer I wanted. "He works here, honey."

"We can't go in there because we don't work here," added my dad, finally getting Adam under control.

Thinking about how cool it would be to feed the flamingos and all the other animals in the zoo, I decided that I wanted to be a zookeeper when I grew up.

Did I become one? No.

It was a dream that faded along with my childhood. Instead, Adam and I became heirs of Fairchild Hotels. Rather than tending to zoo animals, I tend to hotel guests.

When my dad passed away unexpectedly in 2014, I became the CEO of Fairchild Hotels. Adam had fallen on hard times as a teenager, so our dad felt it would be best not to leave him the business. Never in a million years did I think I would become the CEO of anything.

So, what does this have to do with my friend, Ethan Mitchell? The answer is—everything!

Ethan is an example of someone who is passionate about a career at a very young age and actively pursues it. I never pursued zookeeping, but Ethan made homemade movies with his buddies on the weekends. He daydreamed about it when he should have been paying attention in class—except in any biology class.

That's because Ethan was fascinated by both acting and medicine. His mom, who was a doctor, saw this and encouraged Ethan's growing interest in medicine, but she never encouraged his interest in acting.

I never met Ethan until we were both adults. He had already moved to California. Life brought him westward, chasing after his dream of acting. By the time we crossed paths, we were both navigating new careers—Ethan in the entertainment industry and me in the family hotel business. But while I'd left my childhood dreams behind, Ethan's stayed with him through every step.

Now I'll turn it over to Ethan, whose journey to becoming a famous actor—and eventually going down a completely different career path—is quite a story. It's the kind of story only he can tell. As his friend, I've seen Ethan's journey up close.

Now, it's time for you to see it, too—through his eyes.

– **Luke Fairchild**

1

"My action figure is alive!"
"It's trying to kill us!"
"Yeah!"

That riveting dialogue was from the first script I ever wrote. It was cleverly titled *The Action Figure*. The story dealt with a boy's action figure that comes to life, grows to human size, and chases the boy and his friends around the house.

I know, I know—give me a break. I was only nine years old when I wrote it.

A year later, I was in my father's car. We were on our way to Wally's Rental to rent a video camera so we could make the movie. My father, Jeff, would be the cameraman, my friends and I would be the protagonists (or the "good guys," as we had never heard the word 'protagonist'), and our neighbor's oldest son, Jerry, would be the villainous action figure.

While I practiced my lines from the whopping ten-page script, my father was singing along to the songs on a cassette tape he was playing. The tape was a compilation of oldies, mainly from the 1960s. Some songs weren't bad, though I couldn't tell you which ones. I was too busy reading over my script and thinking about how cool it would be to be in a movie.

Well, a homemade movie, anyway.

"Here we are," my father announced as he parked the car. He ejected the cassette tape from the deck before turning off the engine.

It was a nice, sunny, cool September day. There wasn't even a breeze—a quintessential autumn day. Perfect weather to make a homemade horror movie.

We walked inside the store, which wasn't usually busy, even on a Saturday. I followed my father to a counter at the back, where a clerk greeted us with a forced smile. My father gave his name and said he had reserved a video camera.

"I'm making a movie!" I said excitedly. The clerk acknowledged me with a quick nod and half-smile.

While the clerk was getting the video camera, my father noticed some blank video cassette tapes hanging on hooks beside the counter. The shelf above the individual tapes had packs of six. He grabbed one of the blank tapes and set it on the counter.

I neglected to think about having a blank video cassette tape. These are the things a ten-year-old novice filmmaker must remember on shoot day.

After paying for the blank cassette tape and the big, bulky video camera, we left to pick up my two friends. I just hoped my father knew how to operate one of those.

We pulled up to John Bennett's house, where he and my other friend, Mitch Murphy, were waiting. I noticed they were holding copies of the script and had excited looks on their faces. They looked more excited than me.

On the ride back to my house, we practiced our lines and even came up with new ones. John suggested an exchange between his character and Mitch's when we're hiding from the action figure behind the sofa in the living room.

"Shhhh, don't make a sound. It'll find us," John's character would whisper. Then Mitch's character would respond, "Darn, just when I was about to break into song." John was a witty guy, even as a child.

Once we arrived back at my house, I watched as my mother, Susan, carried my four-month-old brother, Alex, out the sliding patio doors. She decided it would be best to stay with Alex in our guest house while we filmed, as she didn't want to disturb us... plus, Alex could suddenly make a noise and ruin a take.

While my father read and tried to understand the instruction manual that came with the video camera, the three of us got everything ready. Not that there was much to get ready—it wasn't like we were using dolly tracks or boom mics.

Jerry arrived shortly after my father had a general idea of how to use the video camera. He had also made a rule that would be strictly enforced, like all the other rules of the house: no fake blood on our clothes, the floor, or the walls. I couldn't blame him. That stuff stained like you wouldn't believe. Getting it off the skin was hard enough. I shuddered to think what would happen if we got it on the white walls or our old wooden doors, which were light brown.

That fake blood would have soaked into the wood, as I remember those doors not being sealed with anything. They were rough, making them more prone to showing fake blood stains.

Jerry brought his costume, which was of my action figure. The action figure itself was the main villain of a cartoon show we used to watch religiously. We liked the villain more than the hero.

A lot more. The villain seemed more interesting—and likable—than the hero, the person we were supposed to be rooting for.

The show was called *School Daze*, and the villain was Professor Rotten. I can't remember the hero's name or even what the show was about. The hero's name was something like "Agent Frost."

Can you tell how much I enjoyed that character?

Jerry's Professor Rotten costume looked like professionals made it. We're talking about the type of detailed costume you would find at theme parks. He said that he wore it once to a fan convention in Minneapolis, not to go trick-or-treating, as my young, naïve brain initially thought.

The filming of *The Action Figure* went well, considering none of us had ever made a homemade movie before. Despite having lines, all our dialogue was improvised. We still made sure to say the gist of what was in the script. None of us bothered to memorize our lines; reading them out loud a few times wasn't good enough.

One thing I clearly remember from that day was filming the ending. In the script, the three of us shove Professor Rotten out the window. Even while writing the script, I knew that wasn't feasible. We would need a stunt performer, a stunt bag (and a means to blow it up), and breakaway glass for the window.

Yeah, that wasn't going to happen.

Instead, we settled on a different way to kill the villain—an "alternate ending," if you will.

We would shove him down the stairs. He would presumably die from a broken neck, as funny as that sounds. An action figure that was not only sentient but now inexplicably the size of a teenager would die from a broken neck. Who cares if it came to life by a spilled chemical?

Using old newspapers lying around the living room, we stuffed them into the costume after Jerry took it off. Jerry knelt on the stairs behind the wall, holding the stuffed Professor Rotten costume. The head was on but wasn't secured to the body. I suggested we use duct tape, but Jerry refused, saying it would likely ruin his costume.

A costume that I later learned cost him close to $200!

"Action!" I yelled, and we ran to the costume and shoved it.

That was Jerry's cue to stop holding it up. We watched as the costume fell backward and landed on the stairs. It didn't tumble down like we thought it would. It just lay on top of the stairs.

The three of us held back laughter as we watched the head tumble down the stairs like a defective Slinky. It landed at the bottom with a small thud. Silence.

"Cut!" I yelled, and my father stopped recording.

All of us burst into laughter, including my father.

"That's a wrap!" I called, and all of us applauded. "Now, let's watch it!" I said.

My mother returned with Alex, and the seven of us watched *The Action Figure*. It was essentially what you would expect from a homemade movie made by a bunch of amateurs. The first indication was the opening credits and how our names were scrawled on a small blackboard with white chalk. Of course, we all laughed at Professor Rotten's death scene, remembering what we went through while shooting. It was funnier when, at the bottom of the screen, we saw the feet of the costume sitting on top of the stairs, pointing up. It always cracked me up.

Alex, being a baby, was indifferent. He alternated between chewing on his teddy bear and picking his nose.

Before driving them home, my father made John and Mitch a copy of the movie. Jerry gave my father a respectable "No thanks" before walking home, carrying his Professor Rotten costume in a large duffel bag.

Filmmaking was never a passion of mine. Later, once acting went from a hobby to a full-blown career, I was interested in working behind the camera. But as a child, I just wanted to act. Making *The Action Figure* didn't satisfy my appetite for acting.

The acting bug bit me, and its venom continued to course through my veins. Despite having written a few other scripts—the shortest being four pages and the longest being twelve—I realized that making homemade movies was only good if I wanted to be a filmmaker, not an actor.

What could I do? I asked my parents, but I only got a shrug of the shoulders. A lawyer and a doctor wouldn't know how to break into acting anyway. I'm unsure why I asked them specifically, but it was worth a shot.

The best I could do for the time being was raise my hand whenever my teacher asked the class who was interested in playing a role in one of our many school plays.

Sometimes I would get a part. Other times, one of my classmates would be slightly quicker at raising their hand.

2

I had never seen snow on Halloween. It was the first and only time I had seen snow that early.

Usually, in Minnesota, we don't see significant snowfall until November. The exception was October 1991, when we not only had snow but a blizzard! By the time John, Mitch, and I went trick-or-treating, about eight inches had already fallen.

It was hard to tell the difference between the road and the ditches. At least one of us was waist-deep in what felt like cold, wet cement. For those who don't know, snow can come in two forms: powdery and wet. The snow will be powdery if the temperature from the ground to the sky is below freezing. It'll be damp and heavy if it's above freezing or above the ground.

As kids, we didn't care if it was snowing—we wanted free candy, and dressing up to get it was a blast. I went as an Eskimo, a last-minute decision since I knew we'd have to wear parkas, snow pants, and boots. My costume was my winter school outfit, recycled for the night.

John went as a zombie, or considering the weather, a zombie Eskimo. He asked his parents if he could rip up his parka and snow pants. Like any reasonable parents, they refused. "It was worth a shot," he told me when he got to my house.

Because of the weather, John's and Mitch's parents told them they could spend the night and go to school with me the next day. In addition to their costumes and snow gear, they just had to pack a change of clothes.

Mitch went as the Grim Reaper, complete with a skeleton mask and a cheap plastic sickle. He had a robe but ditched it because he'd be wearing a parka. Though we rarely saw cars that night, whenever one passed us, Mitch would stare at the driver through his skeleton mask and ominously point at them.

He was such a little prankster, and we always found it hilarious.

We nearly made it through the whole neighborhood before the snow got worse, and we were tired of falling into ditches and being buried in snow. Our candy bags were getting heavy, too.

So, we decided to head back to my house. All we could think about was diving into our candy stash and warming up in the living room.

That's when we saw an SUV coming down the road. Mitch got ready for his pointing gag. But as the SUV approached, we realized something was wrong—it wasn't just moving fast; it was heading straight for us!

"Look out!" I shouted, and we all belly-flopped into the nearest ditch.

The SUV barely missed us. It crushed Mitch's bag of candy, which was lying on the road. That's when I realized the driver hadn't been aiming at us. They had lost control on the snow-covered road.

We watched the SUV veer into a speed limit sign and careened into a ditch. After that, everything went quiet. The wind howled, drowning out the hum of the SUV's engine. The taillights cast a faint red glow over the tire tracks it left in the snow, and the headlights shone weakly on a snow-covered yard decorated for Halloween.

We scrambled out of the ditch, brushing the snow off ourselves. Our candy was scattered all over the road, but none of us cared anymore. An SUV had almost plowed us down!

We stared at the vehicle, waiting for the driver to climb out. But no one did.

"We should check if they're all right," I suggested.

John nodded, but Mitch was still fuming. "Seriously? That person almost killed us!"

"It wasn't on purpose," John pointed out.

John and I were halfway to the SUV when Mitch begrudgingly followed us. "Strength in numbers," he muttered, though I didn't understand why he was suddenly so nervous. It was an accident.

At least, I thought it was.

We reached the driver's side window and peered in. Inside, we saw an elderly man slumped over the steering wheel, unconscious, his mouth hanging open.

"What is it?" John whispered from behind me.

"It's an old man," I said quietly. "He's not moving."

I knocked on the window, hoping to rouse him, but he didn't stir. I tried the door—it was locked.

"What now?" Mitch asked, his bravado fading as he stared at the man slumped in the seat.

Suddenly, the seriousness of the situation hit me like a ton of bricks. This wasn't some joke, and the old man wasn't going to snap out of it. Panic rose in my chest as I realized we might have been the only ones who could help him.

After running back home to get my mother, she smashed the SUV's back window and climbed inside. John and Mitch had stayed behind with the unconscious man while I raced to get her.

Once inside the car, my mother leaned over the seat, checking the man's pulse and breathing.

"Sir, can you hear me? Wiggle your fingers if you can hear me," she said gently, though the man's pale fingers didn't budge. His pulse was faint, and his breathing was shallow.

Before leaving the house, my mother had called 9-1-1. She told the dispatcher she was a doctor and would see what she could do. Even with her medical knowledge, though, there wasn't much she could do for the man beyond forcing an aspirin into his mouth and starting CPR.

As we sat back at my house, John, Mitch, and I ate our "blizzard candy," trying to ignore the tension. We were just kids, after all. But something had shifted in me. I couldn't stop thinking about that man.

After the paramedics came and took the man to the hospital, my mother returned and sat down with us. I knew a heart attack was serious, but not much else.

"What's a heart attack? Like, what happens?" I asked her.

My mother smiled softly, then grabbed a small box of Dots from my candy pile. "A heart attack happens when something blocks your blood from reaching the heart," she explained, her voice calm and measured. As she continued explaining the process in simple terms, I listened intently.

John and Mitch listened, though their minds were still on their candy. They weren't interested in medicine. I wasn't either—at least, not until now.

"Is that what Grandma died of?" I asked.

My mother shook her head. "No, she died of cardiac arrest."

"Don't they both have to do with the heart?"

"They do," she said, "but they're two different things. Cardiac arrest happens when your heart stops beating. A heart attack is when your heart keeps beating but is starved of blood."

As she spoke, something stirred in me. I felt a flicker of curiosity that I couldn't quite explain. That night, I had the sudden urge to learn more about cardiac arrest. I couldn't let it go.

And that's when my fascination with medicine began. The more I read, the more interested I became. And as my interest in medicine grew, my desire to act faded.

Eventually, the acting bug's venom would be fully neutralized.

But looking back, I think about how that moment and my mother's calm, knowledgeable demeanor had planted the seeds of responsibility and compassion in me. Maybe it's why, in later years, I felt such a strong sense of duty to my family—why losing them hit so hard. If only I could've been as calm and as capable when the real tragedies struck. Perhaps I wouldn't have felt so helpless.

That Halloween night was the first time I realized how much one moment, one action, could change someone's life. It wouldn't be the last.

3

You know how when kids learn a new word, they use it all the time?

That's what I did as my knowledge of medical terminology grew. Pee became urine, poop was feces, snot was mucus, spit was saliva, and puke was vomit.

And the medical term for a heart attack? Myocardial infarction. Of course, as a ten-year-old, I called it a "mayocardial infraction." My mom never bothered correcting me—she got a kick out of it. And to be honest, I never referred to it as a heart attack again.

Acting was still an interest, but it had taken a backseat. Even the content in the scripts I wrote changed. No more haunted houses or alien invasions—now, my stories had medical themes. One script was about an expired athlete's foot spray (yes, really) that turned into a weird orange slime, eventually morphing a guy into an orange blob monster.

Another script was about the final days of a man dying from—wait for it—salmonella. Sure, it's life-threatening, but would it make a serious drama? Definitely not. But hey, I was a kid.

My mom was thrilled with my new obsession with medicine. She didn't care much about the crummy scripts, but she thought it cute that I tried to work in medical themes. She'd bring home pamphlets and brochures from the hospital for me to read daily.

Yes, that was my request.

For birthdays and Christmases, I asked for presents related to medicine—primarily books. But my parents got me a microscope one Christmas when I was twelve.

That thing and I became inseparable. I examined everything under it: bugs, dirt, sawdust, even sand. One time, I smeared a sample of my poop on a slide.

Yes, it was disgusting.

Yes, it was extreme.

Yes, I gagged a little, just like you probably did.

But you know what? It was cool.

John and Mitch didn't share my newfound interest. They weren't even that into filmmaking, though they thought being on camera was fun. They kept asking when we'd turn one of my scripts into a movie, but it depended on whether my parents could host, operate the camera, or didn't have plans for the weekend.

At the time, I had no clue what it was like to work more than 40 hours a week and just wanted to relax on weekends. Sometimes, I'd complain, but other times, I'd shrug it off and go back to my microscope or read through my growing collection of medical literature.

Still, making movies or reading wasn't all I wanted to do. I'd hang out with John and Mitch, ride bikes, watch movies, or go to the mall. You know, normal things kids our age enjoy.

One Saturday, my dad dropped me off at the mall to meet with John and Mitch. "Be back at the main entrance by four," he said. This was before cell phones, so I had to watch the time carefully. When my dad said four, he meant it.

I had a plan: I would buy a birthday gift for my little brother Alex and then hit the arcade. Alex was obsessed with Sesame Street, so I figured a plush Big Bird would be perfect.

"Let's go to the arcade!" John kept saying, nagging me since we walked in.

I wanted to get Alex's gift first—just in case I blew all my money at the arcade.

"Trade in any tickets you win for a prize," John suggested. "You'll play, and Alex will get something cool."

I was good at arcade games like skeeball and pinball, but the prizes were usually cheap. The cool prizes required hundreds of tickets, and what if I barely won any? I couldn't give Alex a plastic ring that would break when he put it on.

"No, I want to get Alex something he'll like," I said, shaking my head.

We made our way to the toy store's second floor. Luckily, I found a Big Bird plush that cost most of my allowance, but I still had enough for some arcade fun. The only thing that worried me was what people would think of a 13-year-old buying a Big Bird doll.

"Next stop, the arcade!" John said, clearly thrilled.

"Yeah, now you can shut up about it!" Mitch teased, though I knew it was all in good fun. We'd been friends for so long that breaking us apart would take something big.

To get to the arcade, we had to head downstairs. As we rode the escalator, I noticed a huge crowd gathered around the entrance to a conference center.

It wasn't unusual for special events to happen there, but I was curious.

After stepping off the escalator, I glanced at the sign. A casting call—for a movie being filmed in Minnesota. My heart nearly jumped out of my chest.

"You comin', Ethan?" Mitch asked, heading toward the arcade.

"Go ahead, I'll catch up," I replied, my eyes glued to the crowd.

John was skeptical. "You'd rather stand in that long line than play at the arcade?"

"Yeah," I said. "I'll catch up. Go on."

John and Mitch shrugged and headed toward the arcade. But I wasn't interested in skeeball or pinball anymore. I needed to know more about this movie.

I approached one of the staff members, who was almost lost in the sea of aspiring stars.

"Excuse me, what movie is this for?" I asked.

"It's called *Locked In*. It's a medical drama about a viral outbreak in a juvenile hall," she answered with a smile.

Not only could I audition for a movie, but it was a medical drama!

"Would you like to audition?" she asked.

"Yes!" I could barely contain my excitement.

"Are your mom, dad, or legal guardian here with you?" she asked.

I shook my head. "I'm here with my friends."

She gave me an apologetic smile. "Sorry, sweetie, but you can't audition without a parent or guardian here."

My heart sank. I was on the verge of tears but fought to hold them back.

With no other option, I headed for the arcade, each step weighed down by disappointment. I imagined the casting director telling me, "You would've been perfect for the lead, but you didn't have a parent with you. Better luck next time."

At that moment, something caught my eye—a payphone bank. I raced toward it, fishing out a few quarters. I dialed my home number, and my dad picked up.

"Dad, could you come down to the mall? There's a casting call for a movie, and I want to audition, but I need a parent here," I said, my excitement returning.

But my hopes were quickly dashed.

"Sorry, champ, but your mom was called into work, and Alex still isn't feeling well," he said.

I'd completely forgotten Alex was sick. Mom had found him lying in his own vomit that morning, and he'd been running a fever ever since.

"Can't you get a babysitter?" I asked.

There was a pause, followed by my dad's sigh—a clear sign he was trying to stay calm. "Ethan, the answer is no. Maybe tomorrow."

Tomorrow.

But today was the last day of the casting call. "Please, Dad?" I begged, even though I knew he wasn't going to budge.

"I gave you my answer, Ethan. Now go have fun with John and Mitch. I'll pick you up in a few hours," he said before hanging up.

I stood there, listening to the click of the phone hanging up, feeling like I'd just lost out on something big.

With a sigh, I looked down at the plastic shopping bag in my hand. Big Bird stared at me, reminding me of Alex and how much he'd love his birthday gift. That thought brought a smile to my face.

It didn't erase the disappointment, but it helped.

4

Seeing that casting call at the mall made the dormant acting bug venom course through my veins again.

Acting had always been an interest of mine, but never a major one. Medicine still fascinated me, and I read everything I could. Sometimes, I'd ask my mom if I could go to work with her on weekends if she was called in.

The answer was always no, but I persisted. Later, I realized why. For one, patient privacy, and for another, I'd probably just get in the way.

Acting and medicine—two completely different paths. One seemed more realistic, especially for a kid living in Minnesota with zero connections to the entertainment industry.

Going to medical school and becoming a doctor made more sense, according to my mother. Moving to Los Angeles to chase an acting career? That was risky, mainly because it's so competitive. Dreams don't pay the bills, she'd say, and I'd have to wait tables or work part-time while going to auditions.

Auditioning didn't pay. Then again, neither did job interviews at clinics or hospitals, but at least those didn't depend on how you looked or whether you could recite lines from a script.

The more I thought about it, the more exhausting it became—this back-and-forth between acting and medicine. But whenever my teacher asked for volunteers for a school play, my hand shot up before she could finish the sentence.

By the time I got to high school, I'd signed up for the drama club. I landed roles ranging from the lead to unnamed characters like "Police Officer#3."

But my fondest memory wasn't from high school—it was when acting and medicine collided in the best possible way.

It was April 1998, just before Easter, and spring break was right around the corner. My mom came home from work that Friday, beaming. My dad and I thought she'd gotten a promotion or maybe treated one of the Timberwolves or Vikings players.

Instead, she walked in with an excited smile.

"Ethan, I pulled a few strings and got you a job for this summer!" she said.

I couldn't believe it—I would finally work in medicine. No more driving around and filling out job applications!

"Cool! What is it?" I asked.

"You're going to be a standardized patient! You need to go through training first," she explained, nodding like I knew exactly what that meant.

I didn't.

"What's a standardized patient?" I asked.

"Oh, Ethan, you act like a patient to help teach medical students how to interact with real patients," she said. "That's a brief summary. There's more to it."

Oh. My. God. An acting job involving medicine!

That casting call at the mall suddenly felt like ancient history. Sure, I didn't get to audition for *Locked In,* but I already had the job here. All I needed was training, and I was confident I'd handle it. I'd learned to operate a cash register in a day at the local supermarket—this would be easy in comparison.

But I knew this was different. Being a standardized patient meant memorizing a script, letting medical students question me like an actual patient, and providing feedback on their performance.

Around the time I started training, Alex and I grew closer. He was eight, and we were finally able to hang out more. In the past, our ten-year age gap limited what we could do together, but that didn't stop me from playing board games with him or giving him piggyback rides around the house.

"Wanna ride on the Human Rollercoaster, buddy?" I'd ask, and Alex would nod wildly, laughing as I carried him around.

But as he got older, we did more "grown-up" things—like fishing and playing basketball. Basketball was our favorite, even though the nearby lake wasn't great for fishing.

One day, we were at the park, shooting hoops. We never tried to steal the ball or block each other's shots—it wouldn't have been fair. Instead, we took turns practicing layups, free throws or standing further away to see who could make the furthest shot.

Alex always made more baskets than I did. He was great at basketball, playing it competitively through middle and high school.

We'd also play "Horse" and have little contests where we'd try to outdo each other with fancy shots. This was where I usually excelled.

"Watch this, man," I said, dribbling the ball a few times.

Alex stood there in his t-shirt, shorts, and white tennis shoes, squinting against the sun with his hand acting as a makeshift visor.

I ran up for a layup, the ball going in. I caught it, dribbled a few more times, and stepped away from the basket. Facing forward, I granny threw the ball behind me.

"Cool!" Alex said.

Translation: I made it.

"Got a better one, buddy?" I asked, smiling.

"Yeah, watch!" he said, dribbling as best he could, even though the ball looked huge in his hands. It reminded me of a small child carrying a watermelon in a supermarket—a sight that always made me laugh.

Alex stood by the three-point line, dribbling before taking a shot. The ball went in.

"Great shot, man!" I held up my hand for a high-five.

He ran up, jumped surprisingly high, and slapped my hand before grabbing the ball as it bounced behind the basket near the fence.

Then it happened.

As Alex ran toward the ball, he tripped and slammed into the rusty pole of the hoop. The sound of his head hitting the metal was like a cantaloupe hitting a tiled floor.

For a split second, I froze. My brother had just taken a nasty fall, and I was standing there, staring in disbelief. Then the horror hit me like a wave—Alex wasn't moving.

"Alex!" I screamed.

I ran to him, dropping to my knees so fast that I scraped them on the concrete. I didn't even feel it.

He had a pulse, thank God, but he was unconscious. A thin stream of blood trickled down his forehead.

"Help! Somebody help!" I shouted, but the park was empty. The playground next to the court was deserted, and even the nearby tennis court was vacant. It was early, but not that early.

I tried to comfort Alex, patting his arm. "Stay with me, buddy," I muttered, even though I knew he couldn't hear me. My brain was racing, stuck in fast-forward.

I ran to the road, hoping to flag down a car. The nearest house was a block away, but it felt like it was in another state.

A car approached, and I jumped up and down, waving my arms.

"Get outta the road, dumbass!" the driver yelled as he sped by.

I stood there, defeated, watching the car disappear around the corner. "Minnesota Nice," they say. More like "Minnesota Nice... when it's convenient."

I ran back to Alex and rechecked his pulse. Still there. Thank God.

Looking back, what I did next was reckless, but I had no choice. I had to get help, but I couldn't leave Alex alone.

I slipped my arms under him, one across his back, the other under his knees. Taking a deep breath, I lifted him as carefully as possible, praying I wouldn't lose my balance.

Blood dripped from his head, leaving small crimson circles on the concrete where he'd been lying. I had to hurry.

Cars passed by every now and then, but no one stopped. Maybe they thought we were messing around.

When I reached the sidewalk, I stopped to catch my breath. The house felt miles away, and the basketball court seemed even further.

It was turning into the longest walk of my life.

5

Alex sustained two gashes to the head and a moderate concussion.

That's what the doctor told my parents and me after what felt like an eternity of waiting. At that moment, my desire to become an actor faded away.

I was done with training to be a standardized patient. Instead, I'd meet one in the future—but not as a fellow actor—as a medical student.

Even if I'd still wanted to be an actor, I would've quit to be with Alex. He was only eight years old, and he must've been terrified waking up in a hospital bed surrounded by strangers.

"Can we see him?" my mom asked.

The doctor nodded, and we were led to Alex's room. I sat beside him, holding his hand while our parents took turns reassuring him that everything would be okay. I apologized repeatedly, but Alex waved me off each time with a slight motion of his hand or head. His way of saying, "It's cool."

When visiting hours ended, I didn't want to leave. I begged the nurse to let me stay overnight in case Alex got scared. It took my mom, dad, Alex, the nurse, and eventually the nurse threatening to call security (because I'd started making a scene) to get me to go.

The following day, Alex was released, and we brought him home—relieved and thankful.

***

In September 1999, I started at Willow Park Academy in southwestern Minnesota, not far from the borders of South Dakota and Iowa. The area was flat, with farms stretching out in all directions. It was funny—such a prestigious school, complete with an amazing BS/MD program, located in what we city kids called "the middle of nowhere."

Willow Park Academy wasn't my first choice. I'd applied to Johns Hopkins, the University of Minnesota, and Baylor and was rejected by all three.

But ultimately, it didn't matter where I earned my Bachelor of Science and Doctor of Medicine degrees, as long as

I got them. The important thing was being accepted into Willow Park, mainly because their BS/MD program saved me the hassle of applying to medical schools later.

Speaking of which, I should clarify something. While I earned my Bachelor of Science degree, my parents paid my tuition. Contrary to what some articles claimed when I became famous, I didn't earn a scholarship.

My first year at Willow Park flew by. I was laser-focused on getting good grades. During the summer of 2000, I worked part-time as an orderly at the local hospital, Willow Park Medical Center.

Quick PSA: if you're pursuing a medical degree, even as an undergrad, try to get a part-time job in the medical field. It's an excellent learning experience.

Willow Park was also the first time I had a steady girlfriend. Okay, you're probably thinking, "Bullshit. Ethan Mitchell didn't have a girlfriend until college?" No—I said a *steady* girlfriend. In high school, girls came and went. I remember their faces but not their names.

But I remember my college girlfriend, Ellen Baker, clearly. She started the same year I did. Ellen had a tan complexion, wore glasses, and always kept her beautiful brown hair in a ponytail.

Ellen looked like a supermodel trying to look like a nerd. It didn't work.

Dating wasn't easy, though—most of our "dates" involved meeting in the library to study. Comparing notes on biology and chemistry wasn't the height of romance, but we enjoyed each other's company.

The only downside was that Ellen didn't work at the same hospital I did. Instead, she worked in the student bookstore. It paid well enough—not that she needed the money. Her parents were loaded and generously shared their wealth with her.

Ellen didn't have to work. She never had to save up for toys as a kid or get a job to buy a car as a teen. Mommy and Daddy took care of it. But I think working at the bookstore gave her a sense of independence. She never said it, but I could tell.

"I'm one of the guys," she once told me. She wanted to belong, to be her own person. She no longer relied on her parents' money—she had her own income now and, soon, her own medical career.

Like me.

Soon.

"You've never eaten fast food?" I asked her, incredulous, as we waited in line at a McDonald's drive-thru.

Ellen smiled her beautiful, wholesome smile. She didn't even need to shake her head.

"Oh, you're gonna love it," I said.

And she did. To Ellen, sinking her teeth into a Big Mac and crispy fries was better than any fancy dinner.

Sure, fast food wasn't the most romantic—or healthy—option, but it's a lifesaver when you're in college.

Even mundane things like getting fast food felt special because of how little free time we had.

Ellen and I were in the library one night studying for our Biochemistry midterm. It was the second semester of our third year. The place was practically empty, with only thirty minutes left before closing.

"What did you want to be when you grew up?" Ellen asked out of the blue.

I blinked, surprised. How do you get from studying amino acids to asking about childhood dreams?

"I wanted to be an actor," I said, not looking up from my book.

She laughed. "That's cute. Like in movies or on TV?"

"Any medium," I replied, still focused on memorizing the structure of amino acids.

"What made you want to be an actor?" she asked.

It was a good question. One I hadn't really thought about. Why did I want to act? What drew me to it in the first place? I hadn't done anything remotely related to acting until I made *The Action Figure* with John and Mitch that Saturday.

And it wasn't like I had a relative in the business.

Those questions and amino acid structures rattled around in my head for the rest of the night. After about a three-year hiatus, thoughts about acting returned.

The acting bug venom had reactivated.

6

Date nights with Ellen hardly ever involved going to the movies. We'd watch anything—from bloody horror films to cheesy chick flicks.

That night, we went to see *Midnight Stalker*. I stuffed a handful of popcorn into my mouth as a beautiful young woman with long blonde hair, wearing a light blue nightshirt and white panties, sprinted into a house. A masked killer wielding an axe was close behind. She frantically slammed the door and locked it.

The character's name was Tina Jensen, and as I later found out, she'd dyed her hair for the role. Never in a million years did I expect to end up dating a celebrity, let alone Tina. Maybe I'd treat one in a hospital, but dating? That seemed out of reach.

I glanced at Ellen, whose eyebrows were knitted into a disapproving frown.

I knew that look. It wasn't fear or disgust at the gore—she hated the movie. But every time our eyes met, we smiled. It wasn't about the movie; it was about being together. Even when the film was awful, we stayed to laugh at it.

Besides, it was an escape.

Free from studying.

Free from classes.

Free from dorm life.

Free from college altogether.

Soon, that freedom would become my reality. Going back and forth between wanting to be a doctor and wanting to be an actor had become exhausting, like an ever-ending roller coaster.

I knew it was time to get off the ride. That meant quitting school and heading to Los Angeles, but actually quitting school was easier said than done. Mostly because I'd have to tell my parents, which was a step I wasn't ready to take.

It wasn't just quitting school—it was everything that came with it. Once I told them, either by phone or email, that step would become real. I knew I'd eventually do it, but not before I finished my degree.

The funny thing was that I graduated with my B.S. in Biology. At the time, it didn't feel funny at all. I was stressed out of my mind.

I couldn't bring myself to tell my parents. In May, I wished my mom a happy Mother's Day. In June, I called my dad for Father's Day. Both times, I chickened out. A sick feeling twisted in my stomach whenever they mentioned school.

They said the same things, almost like they were in on it together, waiting to see if I'd stick with medical school. Even though they had no idea I wanted to quit, it felt like their words pierced right through me.

"You start medical school this fall! How exciting!"

"Getting ready for medical school?"

"You're one step closer to being a doctor!"

I talked to Alex often—by phone or email—but I couldn't tell him either. Asking him to pass the news to our parents for me would've been wrong. It wasn't fair to make him the middleman.

Instead, I listened to him talk about school. Alex was doing great—A's and B's in all his classes, and some of them were advanced. He was involved in the school newspaper, the physics club, and the math league.

My little brother was smart, and I'd be lying if I said I wasn't a little envious. I got good grades, but not in all my classes, and I definitely didn't take advanced ones.

"Maybe I can drive down sometime for a visit," Alex suggested.

It was hard to say no to that. I wanted to see him, and maybe telling him in person would give me the courage to finally break the news.

But it never happened, not because of some tragedy, but because Alex got a summer job and couldn't take the time off. He'd just turned sixteen and wanted to start saving for college.

Alex worked at a video rental store and later told me he loved it. At least he had a job he enjoyed.

On the other hand, I spent the summer packing and planning my move to L.A. The more I packed, the more I realized I wasn't just leaving my home state—I was leaving my family behind.

In my naiveté, I thought I'd become a working actor in no time and fly back to Minnesota whenever I wanted. I imagined my parents and Alex wouldn't mind that I'd quit medical school once they saw how successful I'd become.

God, I cringe every time I think about it.

The first person I told was Ellen. She had to know, even if it meant risking our relationship.

We sat in a small coffee shop down the street from our apartment in mid-August. Ellen was sipping a mocha latte, and I had black coffee. I remember exactly what we ordered; you'll see why in a second.

"Every year, it feels like textbook prices go up," Ellen said, shaking her head as she set her cup down. She liked her coffee lukewarm. I, on the other hand, needed mine hot.

"I won't be buying textbooks this year," I said, not making eye contact.

Ellen chuckled. "Prices aren't that high." She stopped laughing when she realized I wasn't smiling.

"Ellen, this is hard for me to say…" I began.

"You're breaking up with me?" she interrupted, already choking up. I hadn't given her any reason to think that, but here we were.

"I don't think a long-distance relationship will work," I admitted, finally meeting her eyes.

"Long-distance? Where are you going?"

"I'm moving to L.A." I looked down again, bracing for her reaction.

There was no laughter. No smile. Just stunned silence.

"What do you mean, you're moving to L.A.? Have you lost your mind?" she snapped, glaring at me. Her hands waved so wildly that I half expected her to knock over her mocha latte.

"It's something I've been thinking about for a while. I'm tired of going back and forth between medicine and acting," I explained.

"So, you're quitting school to chase the most unattainable career possible?" she asked, incredulous. "You're starting medical school in a couple of weeks! You're so close to earning your degree and thinking about throwing it all away?"

Ellen was smart and sweet, but good Lord, she was terrible at motivation. Becoming a doctor wasn't a short road—four years of medical school and another three to seven years of residency—it would take a long time.

But I appreciated what she was trying to do.

"Acting isn't unattainable," I countered.

"Bullshit. You know the joke, right? 'So, you're an actor? At what restaurant?'" she said, rolling her eyes.

"I'm not saying I'll become famous the second I get to L.A. It'll take time."

"You know how expensive it is to live in L.A.? Hell... in all of California?" she shot back.

Looking back, she was right. Living in L.A. was expensive. But at that moment, I was determined.

"I'm quitting medical school and moving to L.A. to become an actor," I said. "I'm sorry I didn't tell you sooner."

Ellen didn't respond. Instead, she picked up her mocha latte and threw it in my face. "Fuck you," she spat before storming out.

And just like that, I lost my first real girlfriend. Unlike my high school relationships, it hurt, which came and went like summer thunderstorms.

But the pain from losing Ellen was nothing compared to what came next.

After changing clothes back at the apartment, I emailed my mom to tell her the news. I figured I couldn't feel any worse.

I was wrong.

The next day, I received her reply:

Ethan,

I got your email and can't believe your foolishness! Quitting medical school to chase your dream of some hollow acting career in Los Angeles is beyond infuriating!

Your father and I sacrificed everything to support your education. Now you've wasted all that time and money for what? A fleeting chance at fame? Do you not realize how selfish and irresponsible that is?

The entertainment industry is a cesspool of superficiality and the odds of making it are laughable. You've turned your back on a real future of helping people, which is an absolute tragedy.

If you persist on this delusional path, don't expect any support from your father or me. You'll be alone, facing the consequences of your travesty of an idea.

I encourage you to think long and hard about your decision and grow the hell up before it's too late.

Mom

She was livid. So was my dad. He wouldn't speak to me for years.

I thought reading that email would lift the weight off my shoulders, but instead, I felt worse. No one supported my decision—Ellen, my parents, even a few professors I'd grown close to over the years.

One, Dr. Schneider, looked like he was holding back tears when I told him. "You had such promise," he said quietly.

The only thing that gave me the strength to pack my bags and drive 1,700 miles to Los Angeles was an email from Alex. He sent it that night, right after I'd read my mom's. His message was short, but it made all the difference:

Hey Ethan,

Mom and Dad just told me the news. As you already know, they're not happy. But I think you already know where they stand.

I want to say I support you 100%. I'm not saying this to make you feel better, but I honestly think you'd be a great actor, just like I thought you'd be a great doctor.

So, I wish you well as you start this new journey. Just promise me you won't do porn. Not because it's trashy, but because I doubt they make microscopic camera lenses. Kidding, kidding.

But seriously—dude, you've got this. Best of luck. I know you'll do great, and I love you. Now, get out there and show these A-listers how to act!

Alex

Alex's email made me cry. I hadn't sobbed like that in years.

I went to bed early that night, emotionally drained but ready to start fresh.

Surprisingly, it wasn't hard leaving the apartment. After packing everything into my 1999 Chevy Cavalier, I took one last look inside. I imagined my new apartment in L.A. would be bigger and brighter, with floor-to-ceiling windows and a view of the Pacific Ocean.

That vision stayed with me on the drive from Minnesota to California.

The weather was beautiful, the traffic wasn't bad, and my car ran perfectly. I barely looked in the rearview mirror—the past no longer mattered. The future was what I was interested in, and it was ahead of me.

I pictured myself as a successful actor. Owning a house on the ocean. Starring in a popular TV show. Dating a famous actress.

That future felt within reach.

But when I arrived in Los Angeles, the only thing I felt was dread.

I wasn't the star of a TV show. I didn't own a house on the ocean.

I was a homeless, unemployed, wannabe actor in a strange city.

And for the first time, I didn't feel like something.
I felt like nothing.

7

Long Beach was stunning. The sun shone brightly, but a gentle breeze kept the heat from becoming overwhelming.

Sitting on the sand, I stared at the waves as they rushed toward me. The water receded and pulled back into the vast Pacific just before they could touch my toes. Further out, surfers rode the waves, and closer to shore, children darted in and out of the water, their laughter carried on the wind.

It hit me then—those people most likely had homes. Real homes. Apartments or houses, not alleys or cars like me. At that moment, the only place I could call home was where I sat on the beach.

Whenever I tried to stand up, my legs felt paralyzed. It wasn't from sitting too long—it was fear. The horrifying realization that I was homeless weighed me down, making it hard to move.

Eventually, I pulled myself up, slipped on my sandals, and walked to my car, parked a short distance away. As I drove around L.A., I expected the dreaded traffic, but sticking to the backroads made it bearable. Finding a place to live was more complicated than I thought. Everything was either too expensive or in terrible neighborhoods. I'd decided long ago, on my drive out here, that I wouldn't settle for a dangerous area, but my options were limited.

After aimlessly driving for most of the day, I found a run-down motel just off Santa Monica Boulevard. The neighborhood wasn't great, but the room had a bed, a bathroom, and locks on the door. That's all I cared about.

It was cheap enough, too.

The room was basic—two queen beds, a small bathroom with a tub/shower combo, and a dresser with an old TV. It wasn't much, but it was better than sleeping in my car.

Ideally, I wanted a studio apartment, but even the smallest ones were too expensive. I could afford rent through the end of the year, but that didn't include food or bills. I'd need a roommate.

And a job.

There were a few restaurants nearby, but none were hiring. I had a vague notion of working on Rodeo Drive in Beverly Hills, imagining I'd make good money as a sales clerk. But first, I needed food.

I stopped at a Mexican restaurant that caught my eye and ordered two chicken enchiladas with cheesy sauce, a side of refried beans, and rice. As the waitress poured water, I asked, "Are you hiring?"

She smiled brightly. "Yes, sir! We're looking for help. Want an application?"

"Absolutely," I replied, relieved at the possibility of employment.

As I filled out the application, I realized I had no permanent address—just a motel. The last thing I needed was to be rejected because I was technically homeless.

While I waited for my food, I became aware of the vibrant atmosphere around me—the sizzling fajitas, the smell of cilantro, and the waitstaff expertly navigating the busy restaurant. I was lost in thought when a woman suddenly slid into the booth across from me.

"Hi there, handsome. Mind if I join you?"

I saw a stunning woman with long, curly hair and dark, seductive eyes. She wore a tight red dress, and her lips were painted a deep shade of burgundy.

"Uh, sure," I stammered, caught off guard.

"My name's Sophia," she said, extending her hand.

I shook it, feeling a jolt at her touch. "I'm Ethan."

"I noticed you filling out that job application," she said, leaning closer. "Are you looking for work?"

I nodded, suddenly self-conscious. "Yeah, I just moved here. Trying to find something."

Sophia smiled, her teeth perfect and white. "Well, I'm looking for someone to work for me."

My heart skipped a beat. Was this woman offering me a job? "What kind of work?"

Sophia leaned back, crossing her legs. "I run a business that requires discretion... and a certain skill set."

I raised an eyebrow, unsure what she meant.

"You ask a lot of questions, don't you?" she teased.

"Sorry, I'm just curious," I said, feeling a bit embarrassed.

Sophia leaned in again, her eyes darkening with intensity. "I run a high-end escort service. I think you have the looks and charm to be valuable to my business."

I blinked, trying to process what she was saying. "I don't know if I'm comfortable with that kind of work," I stammered.

Sophia placed a hand on my arm, sending shivers down my spine. "Don't knock it until you try it. The pay is good, and you'll spend time with beautiful women."

I swallowed hard, torn between temptation and unease. Could I really become an escort?

Sophia slid a sleek black card across the table as if sensing my hesitation. It had her phone number printed in gold lettering.

"Think about it," she said, her voice low and husky.

Before I could respond, the waitress returned with my food. I thanked her and glanced back at Sophia, who was already on her phone, speaking in a low tone.

I couldn't stop thinking about her offer as I ate my enchiladas. Was I really considering this?

Welcome to California, Ethan!

After my meal, I paid the bill and left the restaurant, the sun setting over the palm trees. I walked to my car, lost in thought. Should I call Sophia? Could I really go through with it?

The first job offer I received in L.A. was to be an escort. It was funny in hindsight, but at the time, I was frustrated. All I wanted was a regular job and a permanent place to live.

Before heading to Rodeo Drive, I rented a P.O. box at the post office. I needed something to put on job applications—no one would hire me if they knew I was staying at a motel. Looking back, I have no idea why I did things backward. Maybe it was the stress of being in a new city and desperately needing stability.

I saw a bar and pulled over. There was no way I could interview while feeling this stressed. I needed a drink to clear my head.

The bar had a quiet, laid-back vibe, dim lighting, and middle-class patrons. I ordered an Old Fashioned and took a seat at the bar.

As I sipped my drink, I noticed a man sit down next to me.

"Hey Bart," the man said.

"Luke. The usual?" asked the bartender.

Luke must've nodded because Bart poured him a drink without another word.

"Are you okay?" Luke asked, glancing at me.

I forced a smile. "I'll live," I said.

Luke looked a few years older than me, dressed in black slacks, a burgundy dress shirt, and a black tie. He had a sport coat draped over the back of his stool. Everything about him said "success."

Welcome to California, Ethan!

"Is something wrong?" he asked again.

I laughed a little. "You a psychiatrist or something?"

Luke chuckled. "No, no. My wife calls me a 'professional problem solver.'"

I smiled. "I'm Ethan," I said, extending my hand.

"Luke Fairchild," he said, shaking my hand with a firm grip.

"So, what do you do, Luke?" I asked.

"I manage *The Oracle*, a luxury hotel off Rodeo Drive," he said, noticing my confused expression.

"How long have you been there?"

"About five years," Luke replied. "Say, you never answered my question."

"Which one?"

"Is something wrong?"

I sighed. "I just moved here from Minnesota. Got in yesterday. I'm staying at a motel and trying to find a job. Things are hectic right now."

Luke listened patiently, nodding in understanding. "Yeah, I don't blame you for feeling stressed."

He took a sip of his drink, and I noticed his gold watch for the first time. I wondered if he bought it from one of the shops on Rodeo Drive.

"Just hoping I find a job soon," I added.

Luke thought for a moment. "If you're interested, I could put in a good word with Bob. He manages one of my hotel's restaurants."

I perked up, trying to stay calm. "That would be great, Luke. Thanks."

True to his word, Luke introduced me to Bob Wilson, and I got a job washing dishes at *Tranquility*, the hotel's upscale restaurant. It wasn't glamorous, but it was a start.

I also became friends with Luke—a friendship I'm grateful for to this day.

Tranquility was a high-end restaurant with dim lighting, floor-to-ceiling windows, and polished marble floors. The tables had white cloths, mahogany chairs, and floral centerpieces. It was the kind of place where you knew the profits were huge just by looking at the décor.

The work was tough, but I got to know some of my coworkers, including Joe, the head waiter. We became close, and a month later, I moved in with him.

Within a month of arriving in L.A., I found a job and a permanent place to live.

Now came the "fun" part—the reason I moved herein the first place.

8

If I'd wanted to be a model, I could've called myself successful just a few months after moving to L.A.

I met Connor Lewis one night at *Tranquility*. It was a busy Friday, and I was pulling double duty as a busser and dishwasher. Despite two other dishwashers working with me, the night was hectic. As I loaded a gray plastic bin full of dirty dishes, I noticed a heavyset man sitting at the bar, staring at me. His gaze was so intense that I felt it burn through me. But I had work to do, so I ignored it.

"Excuse me," a voice called out, followed by a firm hand on my shoulder.

I turned to see the man—Connor, though I didn't know his name yet—introducing himself. He told me he represented male models and wanted to sign me.

That's how I met the man who helped launch my modeling career. He didn't represent actors, but later, he introduced me to someone who would.

It might sound like I'm skipping ahead, but that's how it happened. Many models and actors get discovered by being in the right place at the right time. I was one of the lucky ones.

Just like that, I started modeling. And man, did I have a lot of jobs.

The one that stood out most was a sleek black sports car. The shoot took place in Victorville, on the southwestern edge of the Mojave Desert, in the middle of summer.

I arrived expecting to wear a tank top and shorts and maybe sit behind the wheel. But the client had other ideas.

They handed me a white tank top, black leather pants, a black leather jacket, socks, and shoes to match. I was going to be decked out in leather under the scorching desert sun.

I figured at least I'd be inside the car with air conditioning. Wrong.

They had me leaning against the car, sitting on the hood, and posing with the door open. I was sweating buckets within minutes. At least the jacket was unzipped, but the heat was brutal.

"Okay, Ethan, let's get some shots of you lying on the hood," the photographer said.

I glanced at Connor, who was on his phone, as usual. He wasn't at every shoot but came to this one for some reason.

I lay on the hood, closing my eyes to block out the sun, even with my expensive sunglasses on.

That's when the itching started. First, a little itch on my arm. I scratched it, but then the itch spread to my neck, back, and legs. Soon, I was frantically scratching all over.

"Ethan, stop itching. We need to shoot," the photographer said, annoyed.

I tried to stay still, but it was no use. The itching was unbearable. I felt like a thousand mosquito bites had erupted all over my body.

"Ethan, I said stop itching," the photographer snapped.

"I'm trying, but I can't help it," I muttered, sitting up to scratch my legs.

Connor walked over, noticing the red bumps on my neck. "What's going on?"

"I don't know, man," I replied, scratching even harder. "It just started."

Connor took a closer look at my arms, covered in red bumps. Hives.

Connor told me to head to the trailer and change out of the leather outfit while he talked to the photographer. Inside, I stripped down and saw hives all over my body. I scratched furiously, trying to ease the discomfort.

Turns out, I was allergic to leather. Strange, because I used to have a leather jacket in college, but I guess it wasn't genuine leather—or maybe I developed the allergy later.

After a call to the client, they agreed to let me wear a tank top and jeans for the rest of the shoot. Much better.

Once I changed, the hives disappeared almost instantly. The rest of the shoot went smoothly, and I left the Mojave Desert knowing that leather and I didn't mix.

A few modeling jobs later, I had enough money to quit *Tranquility*. But I stayed in touch with Luke. Luke even visited the set for *Perfection*, a men's cologne shoot, which I mentioned earlier in this memoir.

Luke was busy with his job managing the posh hotel in Beverly Hills, and he had a wife and two daughters, so we didn't hang out often. But when we did, we kept it simple—drinks, dinner, playing cards—regular guy stuff.

Joe, my roommate and former coworker from *Tranquility*, was another close friend. I didn't know until I moved in that he was also an aspiring actor. He mainly did theater but wanted to break into TV and film.

Helping him practice lines for auditions was fun and a great learning experience. I once asked if he'd ever thought about modeling, but he brushed it off. To each their own, I guess.

One day, Joe invited me to an audition for a teen drama called *Sealed Lips*. He was auditioning for the role of Tommy Hughes, the abusive boyfriend of one of the main characters, Christina—played by none other than Tina Jensen, who I remembered from *Midnight Stalker*, that horror movie I'd seen with Ellen.

I hadn't planned on auditioning. I just went to support Joe. As I sat there, reading a magazine, Joe and the other actors read over their lines. Everyone was dressed for the part, in worn clothes that fit the character.

The casting director stepped out. "Joe Shaffer," she called. Joe stood up confidently, dressed in a tank top and ripped jeans and walked toward her. With his chiseled good looks and strong presence, he looked the part.

I couldn't help but feel a bit jealous.

As Joe headed in, the casting director glanced at me. "Excuse me, sir, are you auditioning?"

I looked up, surprised. "No, I'm just here with my friend."

She gave me a sharp look, almost as if she was sizing me up. Then she turned back to Joe and led him inside.

A few minutes later, Joe returned, looking confident.

"How'd it go?" I asked.

"Pretty well," he said, smiling.

"Excuse me, sir, would you mind coming in?"

I looked up again. The casting director was talking to me.

I followed her into the casting room, which was simple—a fold-out table and a camera on a tripod.

"Please tell me your name and a little bit about yourself," she said.

After introducing myself, I noticed her gaze shift from my face to my chest. It reminded me of Sophia from that Mexican restaurant, only this time, it wasn't about becoming an escort.

A few days later, I got the news: I'd landed the role of Tommy Hughes. After months of modeling, I finally made the jump into acting.

9

To my surprise, Joe was supportive. I thought he'd be jealous or upset, but instead, he clapped me on the back and said, "I'm glad one of us got the part."

Not long after, Joe landed a role in an indie comedy filming in Vancouver. He was gone for about a month, right around the time I started shooting my scenes for *Sealed Lips*.

I didn't meet Tina Jensen until our first day on set. The first scene we had together was intense—my character, Tommy, had to grab her and throw her onto the couch.

The scene started with a knock at the door. "Who's knockin' at my door?" I had to shout.

"Can I see through doors?" Tina, playing Christina, quipped back.

I leaped off the couch, grabbed her, and yelled, "You watch your mouth! You hear me?" before tossing her onto the couch.

It was a difficult scene to get into, especially with someone like Tina, who was not only beautiful but also incredibly accomplished. I couldn't help but laugh, thinking about how Ellen and I had once poked fun at her character in *Midnight Stalker*.

But as an actor, you can't let your feelings distract you. You have to use them, not let them control you. That's something I now teach my acting students.

When playing a villain like Tommy Hughes, you must find something redeemable in the character, some flicker of good. I imagined that Tommy's aggression came from deep internal pain, maybe even a mental condition. It helped me see him as more than just a one-dimensional abuser.

Shooting the scene with Tina was eye-opening. Everyone on set admired her professionalism, and she never took anything personally. As soon as I grabbed her, she went limp, letting me throw her onto the couch just as we had rehearsed with the stunt coordinator.

We shot the scene several times from different angles. Each time, I had to shout and throw Tina around. Despite knowing we were acting, it felt unsettlingly real.

During one take, Tina's arm hit an end table with a loud bang, and she let out a grunt of pain. I flinched, worried I had actually hurt her.

I knelt beside her at lunch as the crew headed toward the taco bar. "Are you okay?" I asked, offering a sheepish smile. "I heard your arm hit that table pretty hard."

Tina smiled back. "I'm fine, Ethan. Promise." She rubbed her elbow, clearly unbothered.

Being my first acting gig, the pressure was intense, especially working alongside Tina. But the scene went off without a hitch, and as I ate my tacos, I couldn't help but marvel at how quickly my dream of becoming an actor was coming true.

It was around this time that Tina and I started dating. In a strange way, the intense scenes brought us closer. We spent more time together, rehearsing to ensure I didn't hurt her during the physical scenes—especially the notorious one where Tommy drunkenly threatens Christina with a belt after finding out she cheated on him with Brian, her soon-to-be love interest.

If you don't remember the scene, Tommy staggers in, his face twisted in rage, waving the belt as Christina scrambles around the room, trying to escape. He corners her in their bedroom, taunting her with a crooked smile before the scene ends with the sound of the belt snapping in the air.

When we wrapped that scene, Tina and I collapsed into each other's arms, laughing so hard our faces hurt. It was strange how quickly we had bonded over two weeks of filming.

Once Tommy's character arc ended with his arrest and Christina moving in with Brian, my time on *Sealed Lips* was over. But Tina and I weren't.

We moved in together soon after—well, technically, I moved into her place.

Tina's house was everything I'd imagined a celebrity home would be: three stories, a sunroom with floor-to-ceiling windows overlooking the Pacific, a patio with a built-in grill, and a pool. No hot tub, but I wasn't complaining. It beat the crummy motel I had been staying in.

Her house was gorgeous, a word I'd only ever used to describe women until then. But it fit both Tina and her home. She had a gentle face with almond-shaped eyes that twinkled when she smiled. Her skin was smooth, her complexion warm, and her thick black hair framed her face perfectly.

One day, I pulled into the driveway and noticed a police car parked in front of the garage. My stomach dropped.

Inside, Tina was sitting on the couch, tears staining her cheeks. Two police officers stood over her. When I walked in, one of them immediately put a hand on his gun, but Tina quickly explained who I was. The officer relaxed, though I didn't.

"What's going on?" I asked, my voice tight.

Tina wiped away her smeared mascara. "I have a stalker."

My heart stopped. "What?"

She had been dealing with this stalker for months, but I had no idea. It started with harmless fan letters and online messages. But then the tone shifted. The letters became threatening. He hated seeing pictures of us in magazines and on TV.

One of the officers handed me the latest letter. My hands trembled as I read it:

"I've been watching you for weeks and know everything about you. I know where you live and who your loved ones are. You might think you're safe, but you're not. I'm always watching. If you don't leave Ethan soon, I'll make sure he's out of the picture. And trust me, you won't escape unscathed either. You will be punished."

The letter was signed *Graham Collins*—the name of Tina's love interest in *Midnight Stalker*.

"What are you doing to keep us safe?" I demanded, my voice shaking.

"We're doing what we can," one of the officers replied, his tone calm but firm. "We don't have much to go on. He's been signing everything with that fake name."

I wanted to scream, to demand they do more. But instead, I sat beside Tina, wrapping my arm around her as she cried into my shoulder.

I suggested we stay at a hotel that night, but Tina insisted on staying at the house. We locked every door and window, but I couldn't shake the feeling that the stalker was watching us, maybe even inside the house. Every creak of the floorboards and every whisper of the wind made my skin crawl.

I barely slept, peeking over the covers at the bedroom door, half expecting to see a shadowy figure lurking there.

You didn't comply, Tina. Now I found you. You know what that means.

I imagined the stalker's voice as a low, raspy whisper, like a snake slithering through tall grass. Those words played over and over in my head.

Somehow, I eventually fell asleep, but the fear never left.

10

I didn't expect to sleep well that night, but surprisingly, staying in bed was easy. The mattress was soft, and even with my back to the big picture window, I could feel the sun's warm rays massaging my bare skin.

The phone rang, jolting me out of my daze. I groaned, trying to ignore it, hoping Tina would get it. But when I rolled over, I realized she wasn't in bed. The phone rang again. With a heavy sigh, I reached over and picked up the receiver.

"Hello?" I mumbled, still half-asleep.

It was Kevin, my agent, and he was his usual enthusiastic self. "Ethan, get down here, man! I've got something for you!"

"What is it?" I asked, yawning into the phone.

Kevin, as usual, wasn't interested in small talk. "Just come to the office. Trust me, you won't regret it!"

Kevin always sounded like a used car salesman when he had potential gigs lined up. But I couldn't deny that he was damn good at his job. I couldn't help but wonder—was it another guest spot on a TV show? I'd done several already since transitioning from modeling to acting. But I wanted more—a lead role in a movie or, better yet, a TV show.

Before leaving, I found Tina in the kitchen, eating cereal on the island. She was still shaken from the stalker's letter, and her eyes were a little puffy from crying.

"Kevin says he has something for me," I said.

Tina smiled, though it didn't quite reach her eyes. "Make sure you go for a test drive before you buy." She had always found Kevin's salesman pitch as amusing as I did.

At Kevin's office, he greeted me in the lobby, practically bouncing with excitement. "Ethan, you're gonna love this!" he said, slinging his arm around me like we were old pals.

Once we were seated in his office, Kevin leaned forward, his grin wide. "How would you like to be the star of a TV show?"

I blinked. "What?"

Kevin went on to explain. The show was called *Country Doctors*, a drama about a group of teens in a small country town who dream of becoming doctors. The lead role, Danny Hayes, was still up for grabs. They had already cast the beautiful Australian actress Laura Preston as the love interest, Patty, and Craig Murray, another Aussie, as Danny's best friend, Tyler. But they hadn't found their Danny yet.

It was my dream role—a combination of acting and medicine. It almost felt like fate.

Kevin suggested I brush up on my Southern accent for the audition. I wasn't sure what made him think I could pull it off, but I wasn't about to argue.

When I walked into the casting room, Patrick Schwartz, the show's creator, sat behind the table with the casting director. I took a deep breath and dove into the scene, surprised at how naturally the Southern accent came to me.

After I finished, Patrick leaned forward, his hands folded. "That was great, Ethan. Where did a Minnesota guy like you learn a Southern accent?"

I chuckled. "Thank you. It just sort of... came to me."

Patrick exchanged a glance with the casting director. "Would you mind sticking around? We have a few more actors to see, but I really liked what I saw."

"Of course," I replied, trying to stay calm, though inside, I felt like a kid on Christmas morning.

As the other actors auditioned, I sat in the waiting area, picturing myself on set, hitting my marks, nailing my lines. I knew I didn't have the role yet, but I couldn't help imagining it.

After what felt like hours, it came down to me and one other actor. He sat across from me, focused on his lines. I didn't bother trying to chat him up. I'd learned my lesson about that back when I first started auditioning. There was this actor who had thrown me off my game by chatting with me right before my audition. He got the part, not me. I wasn't going to make that mistake again.

The casting director finally called the other actor in. I started timing him, another habit of mine. Auditions typically take five to ten minutes, but he was in there for over twenty. My palms began to sweat, my heart racing. Why was I suddenly so anxious? Maybe it was the pressure of being this close to my dream job.

Finally, the door opened, and the actor walked out, laughing with the casting director. My heart sank. *Good work, good work*, I heard her say as they parted ways.

I was next. The casting director called me back in, and I followed her into the room. Patrick stood up from behind the table, a smile on his face.

"Ethan, right?" he said, extending his hand.

"That's right," I replied, slipping back into the Southern accent for no real reason.

Patrick laughed. "I like it," he said, giving me a firm handshake. Then, his tone grew more serious. "We saw some great actors today. The guy who was just here gave a phenomenal audition, but... he doesn't have the right look."

My heart was in my throat. Was I about to get the part?

Patrick smiled. "You, Ethan, have the right look, and I loved your take on Danny. What I'm saying is, you've got the part."

I almost couldn't believe it. "Thank you!" was all I managed to say before leaving the room.

Once in my car, I cranked the air conditioning and leaned back, a huge grin spreading. I'd made it. Sure, I'd already had some TV roles, but this…this was the lead role. This was different.

Tina was ecstatic when I told her the news. She ran into my arms, excitedly shrieking as I spun her around.

"When do you film the pilot?" she asked breathlessly.

"March next year, in Burbank," I said.

"I just know it'll get picked up!"

"Picked up?" I asked, confused.

Tina smiled patiently. "The pilot must be filmed first, then screened for producers and studio heads. If they like it, they'll order more episodes."

Her explanation dampened my excitement a little. I had assumed that landing the role meant I would have steady work, but now I realized nothing was guaranteed. Until the pilot was filmed and picked up by a network, I had to keep auditioning and keep working.

But that was okay. I had gotten my foot in the door, and for the first time, I felt like I was exactly where I was meant to be.

11

Shortly after earning the part of Danny on *Country Doctors*, along with Tina's brief lesson about how television pilots worked, I emailed Alex.

Alex and I hadn't talked in a while. He was busy with school and his part-time job. I was consumed by my acting career. Modeling petered out around the time I auditioned for *Country Doctors*. Since I wanted to focus solely on acting, I told Connor I was parting ways with his agency. He didn't seem too disappointed. It's just how it works in showbiz—things come and go, and so do people.

The day after I emailed Alex, he responded with his usual—and very welcomed—support. I had thrown out an idea about him coming for a visit during Christmas and New Year's, knowing he had a mid-winter break around that time. He loved the idea and said he'd save up for airfare, but I told him not to worry; I'd cover it. My acting gigs had been paying well enough.

According to Alex, our parents liked the idea. I suspected they agreed because it was an opportunity to spy on me. Even if that were true, I wouldn't have minded. As a father now, I would understand.

My parents and I still weren't speaking, which hurt more than I let on. I had Alex pass along my new phone number and address in case they needed to reach me for any reason. They never did, which confirmed what I already knew—they were still angry.

Alex's arrival was set for December 23. In the meantime, I continued acting classes to sharpen my skills. No matter how many gigs you get, there's always room to grow, and I didn't want to lose my edge.

Luke Fairchild and I kept in touch regularly, and sometimes, I even helped out at *The Oracle*. The partnership that grew between us eventually became one of the smartest moves I ever made. When *Country Doctors* became a hit, word got out about my involvement with the hotel. *The Oracle* went from being popular to becoming the "it" place to stay in Los Angeles.

But the night that Tina's stalker reentered our lives is one I'll never forget.

After filming for *Country Doctors* wrapped, Luke threw me a surprise party at *The Oracle*. It was one of those nights that felt like I had finally arrived in Hollywood. I rubbed shoulders with producers, directors, and even a few actors I had admired for years. Laura Preston, my co-star, brought her real estate mogul boyfriend, Andrew Harper, and I remember thinking how surreal it was to be part of this world now.

Tina couldn't join me at the party. She had a red eye to Toronto for as mall movie role, and by the time the party started, she was already at LAX. I remember thinking, as I walked around the party, how far we'd both come since we first met on the set of *Sealed Lips*.

Around two in the morning, I decided to head home. I hadn't had much to drink, knowing I'd be driving. As I walked out to my car, I felt this overwhelming sense of pride. The party, the attention, and the recognition all felt like the culmination of my hard work. But as soon as I turned the key in the ignition, the car sputtered and died.

I tried again. Nothing.

"Of course," I muttered.

With no cell phone on me (because, of course, I left it at home), I headed back inside to ask Luke for a ride. He looked exhausted but nodded when I explained the situation.

The drive home was quiet. Luke and I were too tired to talk, the yawns catching up with us. The streets were still surprisingly busy for the early morning hours, but I didn't think much of it. My mind was on sleep and how the party had gone off without a hitch.

When we pulled up to the house, I noticed the porch light was on, but the front door was slightly ajar. My stomach clenched, but I tried to brush it off—Tina probably just forgot to lock it in her rush to the airport.

I opened the door slowly, just in case. "Tina?" I called softly, not expecting an answer since she should have been long gone.

But then I saw her.

Tina was lying on the marble floor, her body limp, her face partially obscured by her hair. A small puddle of blood had formed beneath her head. I froze. It felt like the air was sucked from my lungs.

"Tina!" I screamed, my legs carrying me to her side before I even processed what was happening.

Luke was right behind me, already dialing 911. I dropped to my knees, lifting her head gently into my lap. Her body was cold, but there was still life—faint, but there.

"Stay with me," I whispered, my voice shaking. "You're going to be okay."

I rocked her gently, trying to hold back the rising panic. Her breathing was shallow, almost imperceptible. Her eyes fluttered but didn't open. My mind raced, but I kept telling her she was going to be fine as if repeating it would make it true.

The police arrived quickly, along with paramedics who rushed Tina to the hospital. I stayed behind with Luke, answering the officers' questions. That's when one of them noticed a notepad on the kitchen island. A note was scrawled across the page: *I'M SORRY*. The handwriting didn't match Tina's.

The dread hit me like a punch to the gut. "It's him, isn't it?" I asked, already knowing the answer.

It was.

The police combed through the house, searching for any sign of the intruder. Tina was already in surgery when Luke and I arrived at the hospital. The waiting was unbearable. I kept replaying the moment I found her, the sight of her blood on the floor, and the note.

Hours later, the police found him. Noel Gustafson, the stalker, had never left the house.

He had broken in, attacked Tina, and then, after his sick attempt, went upstairs to the bathroom, where he slit his wrists and bled out in the tub. The police found him naked in the water, which was a mix of his blood and bathwater. He had been crying, they said.

He didn't leave his clothes behind, and they never found them. He had walked into our house naked, committed those horrors, and then ended his life in the most grotesque way possible.

It was surreal. It felt like a scene from a twisted crime drama, but it was real—too real.

12

Very little sleep was had that night.

Tina was moved into the ICU after her surgery. Despite my pleading with her doctor and the nurses, I wasn't allowed to see her. Luke stayed with me, offering comfort and making trips to get us coffee. The cafeteria was closed, so we had to settle for the bitter brew from the machine.

The night passed in a blur. We were both sitting in the cold hospital waiting room, speaking in hushed tones when we spoke at all. My mind kept replaying the events over and over, twisting thoughts of what could have been done differently.

When morning came, Tina's doctor woke us up. As I rubbed the sleep out of my eyes and tried to adjust them to the harsh fluorescent lights, he spoke the words I hoped I'd never hear.

"Ethan, I'm sorry. She didn't make it."

"What?" I asked, my voice cracking. It wasn't disbelief—I had heard him—but more like my brain needed another moment to process what my heart already understood.

Luke placed a steadying hand on my back, but I barely felt it.

The doctor explained that Tina had suffered a brain hemorrhage. They'd tried everything, but the bleeding was too severe. "It's a complication that can happen post-surgery," he added.

But the specifics of her death didn't matter. Whether it was during surgery, before surgery, or after—she was gone. And the weight of that reality was unbearable. There was no comfort in the explanation. The fact that her life had been ended by the violence of someone else only made it worse.

Luke offered to let me stay with him and his family for a while. I accepted. The thought of returning to that house, the one Tina had made feel like home, was impossible.

In the months that followed, I kept myself busy with work. I took on two guest roles and a small part in a TV movie. The long days on set were a welcome distraction from the silence that greeted me at night. But when the cameras stopped rolling, and the world quieted down, the grief was waiting. There were nights when the only thing

I could do was lie awake, staring at the ceiling, wondering how everything had changed so quickly.

I never went to Tina's funeral. The role I'd landed conflicted with the date, and Kevin insisted I couldn't miss it. I should have been there. I should've been standing with her family, saying goodbye. But I wasn't. I let my career take precedence over something far more important, and I've regretted it every day since. Sending a sympathy card to her parents felt hollow, like a poor substitute for what I should have done.

When the role wrapped, I visited her grave. I needed that closure.

On the day I went, I dressed in black—pants, shirt, the works. I didn't need to, but it felt like the least I could do. I knelt in front of her headstone, laying flowers down carefully, as though even the slightest misstep would undo the moment.

I prayed, even though I wasn't sure what I was asking for. Forgiveness, maybe—for missing her funeral, for not protecting her, for not being there when she needed me most. Then I talked to her. I told her about the projects I'd finished, how Luke had been there for me, and how Alex was coming to visit soon. I said I missed her, thought about her every day, and was sorry for everything.

The cemetery was quiet, the kind of peaceful that feels heavy. A gentle breeze brushed over me, but that didn't break the stillness. It was like the world had pressed pause just for a moment, just for me to say goodbye. But it didn't make it easier.

When Alex arrived at the airport two days before Christmas, I felt something lift for the first time since Tina's death. When I saw him coming down the escalator, I waved like a lunatic, hoping he'd spot me. He did.

Seeing him again was surreal. When I moved to California, the kid I'd left behind had grown into a young man, taller than I remembered, his frame lean but muscular. He wore a black T-shirt and dark jeans, his parka draped over his arm—a remnant of Minnesota's winter. His hair was spiked up, the way I used to wear mine, and his face carried the confidence of someone who had found their stride.

"Hey, man!" he said, dropping his parka and pulling me into a hug.

"Hey, buddy. It's great to see you."

And it was. It was more than great—it was necessary.

As we walked toward the parking garage, his parka now slung over my arm, Alex chattered non-stop about school, his spot on the basketball team, how he was making the honor roll, and even about his girlfriend. I listened, grateful for the noise, for the normalcy. It was the first time in months that I didn't feel the constant ache of grief pressing down on me.

We spent the next two weeks hitting every theme park we could—Disneyland, Knott's Berry Farm, Six Flags. It was the kind of fun I hadn't allowed myself to have since

Tina died, and having Alex there made it easier. His presence was a reminder of life, of family, and how much I still had left despite the emptiness Tina's death had created.

New Year's Eve came faster than I expected. As we counted down to midnight, Alex disappeared into the spare room, emerging with a box wrapped in shiny gold paper.

"Mom and Dad wanted me to give this to you tonight," he said, handing it over.

The box was about the size of a wine bottle, wrapped with precision down to the matching gold bow. I turned it over in my hands, wondering what it could be.

"They don't want you to open it until midnight," he added with a mischievous grin.

We toasted the new year with sparkling cider when the clock struck twelve. I set my glass down and tore into the wrapping paper, revealing a gold plastic statue—an imitation Oscar. My name was engraved on a plaque at the base.

I chuckled and set the statue on the coffee table before noticing an envelope inside the box. While Alex admired the statue, I opened the envelope, unfolding a letter written in my mother's neat handwriting.

The words blurred for a moment as my eyes welled up. I blinked the tears away and began to read.

Dear Ethan,

Today marks the beginning of a new year, but I hope it marks the start of a new chapter for us.

Ever since I saw your acting on Sealed Lips, I realized that you are one talented young man. I wasn't expecting your career to take off the way it has, and it made me reflect on how I reacted when you told us about moving to L.A.

I was wrong, Ethan. I reacted out of fear. I was afraid you'd be alone in a difficult industry, afraid you'd fail, afraid you'd forget us. I'm ashamed to admit it, but my anger came from a place of worry. I never doubted your talent, but I doubted my ability to let you go.

I hope this year brings us a new beginning. I'm proud of you, and I always have been.

Love, Mom

"Ethan? You okay, man?" Alex asked, noticing the tears in my eyes.

I wiped at them quickly, forcing a smile. "Yeah. I'm good."

But I wasn't fooling him. He sat down beside me, throwing an arm around my shoulders. "You sure? I saw the tears."

"It's just this letter from Mom." I handed it to him, watching as he read it and nodding to the words.

That letter is now framed in my office beside the faux Oscar statue. Some might find it corny, but to me, it symbolizes something more profound—the moment my mother finally accepted my choice. It wasn't just a plastic statue; it was a gesture of reconciliation, an acknowledgment of my journey and the courage it required.

And it was one of the best gifts I've ever received.

13

Little did I know I wouldn't see Alex again until 2009. He would be an extra in one of the second-season episodes of *Country Doctors*.

A few months after Alex left, I went to Rising Star Studios in Burbank for the table read. That was when I met my co-stars for the first time. The first person I bumped into was Laura Preston, who played my character's love interest, Patty. One of the first things I noticed was the sweet, fruity scent of her hair.

"Is that strawberries I smell?" I asked, trying to break the ice.

Laura blushed, brushing a strand of her brown hair behind her ear. "Oh, God. Yeah. I ran out of shampoo, so I grabbed whatever I could find at this random drugstore."

She looked a bit embarrassed, but I laughed it off. "Could be worse. I once had to use dish soap."

Her nervous smile turned into a laugh, and just like that, we clicked. Laura had dyed her hair brown for the role since Patty was written as a natural brunette, but even with the dye, she had an effortless charm that made her seem like the perfect fit for the character. We sat next to each other during the meeting, exchanging small talk.

Then *he* walked in. Craig Murray.

Craig was late, muttering something about traffic, but his body language said more than his words. He didn't want to be there. I later learned from Patrick, the show's creator, that Craig had been up for the role of Danny until I auditioned. That explained the cold shoulder and the simmering tension that would grow between us, both on and off the set.

Craig wasn't exactly easy to get along with. He had short, spiky hair that looked like it could double as a weapon and a lean build but without the muscle definition Alex had. He always did pushups between takes, like he had something to prove. When we shook hands for the first time, I smiled and said, "Nice to meet you," but Craig barely managed a nod and mumbled, "Hi." Aloof, as Patrick put it. I would've used a different word, but I wasn't about to stir up any trouble. I didn't want to jeopardize my first lead role.

Looking back now, it's strange how the tension between Craig and me felt like more than just professional rivalry. Something was simmering beneath the surface—a frustration, maybe even resentment—that had nothing to do with the role itself. It was as though Craig saw me as a symbol of something he had lost, something I had taken without even realizing it. We were both too proud to talk about it, though. And in Hollywood, pride is sometimes the hardest thing to set aside.

During the table read, I noticed Laura and Craig both taking notes. Laura, especially, was meticulous—she'd underline certain words, jot little reminders in the margins, and even wrote "CRY" in big letters next to one of her more emotional lines. Watching her work made me realize how much I still had to learn. I started taking notes, too. It became a habit, one I now teach my students.

Patrick sat at the head of the table, watching us with this quiet intensity. He cracked a few jokes, but there was something...off. Even early on, I noticed Patrick wasn't as laid-back as he wanted people to think. It was like there was always something ticking beneath the surface, some internal clock he was racing against. It made me wonder what his true motivations were, even back then. I chalked it up to the pressure of launching a show but looking back, maybe that was my first glimpse of who Patrick really was.

Wanda Richardson, one of the executives at Rising Star Studios, was also at the table read. Wanda had this infectious smile that could light up a room. She was dressed sharply—red blouse, black miniskirt, and matching red stilettos—but she didn't have that untouchable air some execs carry. She laughed at Patrick's corny jokes, complimented our line readings, and made the process less intimidating.

This table read felt different. I'd done guest spots and minor roles before, but this time, it was clear—I'd be working with these people for a while, building something more significant. When we wrapped up the read, I thought, *This is it. This is the beginning.*

And it was. Filming the pilot went smoothly. The chemistry between us was instant—well, mostly. Craig and I managed to act like best friends onscreen, but as soon as the cameras stopped rolling, he reverted to barely making eye contact with me. Still, the show felt special. We all hoped the network would pick it up, but there were no guarantees in this business. It wasn't like being a guest star, where you finish your stint and move on. This was different. If the show got picked up, it meant stability. It meant not worrying about where the next gig would come from.

Laura threw a small party at her house for the premiere, and for fun, we all dressed up like farmers, fitting the show's theme. Even Craig showed up, much to my surprise. I brought along a plush cow as a nod to Danny's job on the dairy farm. That plush now belongs to my four-year-old daughter, by the way.

The party was a blast. Laura and I spent most of the night talking and getting to know each other better. We figured we should, considering our characters' on-again, off-again relationship would be a central part of the show. But it wasn't just for the sake of the characters. Laura and I genuinely clicked. She was easy to talk to, funny, and had a sharp mind. She told me about her interest in psychology, which I found fascinating since my background was in medicine.

Craig, meanwhile, mostly kept to himself. I'd see him watching us from across the room, his drink in hand, but he rarely joined the conversation. At the time, I assumed he was just shy or maybe still bitter about the role. But as the night went on, something about his behavior didn't sit right with me. It was like he didn't know *how* to join in, like he was stuck on the outside, looking in. I wondered if there was more to Craig than I'd given him credit for. Maybe we were both just too stubborn to see it.

Our on-screen friendship grew stronger as the weeks passed, but Craig remained distant off-screen. Yet, there were moments—small ones—where I saw glimpses of the person Craig could be. Once, during a break between scenes, he asked if I wanted to grab lunch. I was so caught off guard that I almost said no, but something in his voice made me reconsider.

That lunch was awkward at first, but as we talked, I started to understand Craig a little better.

He wasn't aloof.

He was guarded. And while we didn't become best friends overnight, that lunch was the first step toward something more genuine. Over time, the tension between us lessened, and though we never talked about the role or the initial coldness, the air between us began to clear.

As for Patrick, the more time I spent with him, the more I realized that his charm had a shelf life. There were days when his jokes fell flat, his compliments felt forced, and his temper flared over the most minor things. It wasn't constant, but those cracks in his persona were becoming harder to ignore. I didn't think much of it back then, but in hindsight, it was a sign of things to come.

14

Shortly after wrapping the first season of *Country Doctors* in April 2008, my mother sent me a book about various outbreaks around the world and how doctors and officials managed to control them.

Since we reconciled at the start of 2007, she'd started sending me books and articles related to medicine—just like she used to when I was a kid.

Her timing couldn't have been better. Between takes on set, I'd flip through that book, eager for a distraction. Around the same time, Kevin landed me an audition for the lead role in a movie called *Day of the Animals*, though you might know it by its theatrical title, *The Craze*. The script was a blend of horror and comedy—a story about a newspaper reporter, Ryan Merrick, who leads a group of survivors, including his veterinarian ex-wife, to safety after a chemical spill drives the local wildlife into a murderous frenzy.

I loved every word of it.

We filmed in North Dakota from May to June 2008, bouncing between Jamestown, Bismarck, and Dickinson. The latter became our temporary home base—small, rural, and with no Four Seasons in sight. That was fine; I'd take a cozy, no-frills hotel room over luxury as long as it was clean.

The film's director, Howard Hiller, was a legend in the comedy world. He'd signed on to *The Craze* because he was captivated by the script's unique take on horror-comedy. And Howard—well, he had a talent for blending gut-wrenching tension with humor that was, as he liked to put it, "piss-your-pants funny."

Howard was like a mad scientist on set, demanding more blood in the most outrageous moments. "More blood, more blood! I wanna see more fucking blood!" he'd yell, his excitement infectious rather than tyrannical. And he was right—the added gore somehow made the scenes even funnier, in that twisted, absurd way only he could pull off.

One particular memory stands out: the tiger scene. If you've seen *The Craze* (and if you haven't, I'm only kidding when I say, "What's wrong with you?"), there's a moment when my character, Ryan, and a newspaper intern,

Zack, are cornered by a tiger at the zoo. The premise is absurd, sure, but filming it was anything but funny.

The tiger in question, a real, live animal, was well-trained, but as the cameras rolled and I backed against the car door, it was hard to remember that fact. The tiger got up close—nose-to-nose with me, teeth bared and growling. The growls were dubbed during post-production, but at the moment, I didn't need sound effects to feel terrified.

"Don't be afraid, Ethan, she's a pussycat," the trainer said casually from off-set.

I wanted to scream, *Why don't you come out here and say that to her face?!* But I stayed quiet, focusing on staying still, very still.

"And... cut!" Howard yelled. The trainer rushed in, and the tiger backed away. We repeated the scene several times, each more nerve-wracking than the last. On one take, the tiger refused to move after the trainer whistled. It stood over me, claws lightly pressed against my legs, ignoring the whistle as the trainer's voice grew more insistent.

"Don't move, Ethan," the trainer called.

Oh, don't worry, I'm not going anywhere, I thought, my heart racing. Closing my eyes didn't help. I could still feel the tiger's claws. Finally, the trainer came over and coaxed the tiger away with a soft whistle.

"Are you okay?" Howard asked, coming over as I slowly opened my eyes.

"Did you get the shot?" I replied, managing a shaky smile.

That story became my go-to anecdote during the press junkets when *The Craze* premiered in February 2009. Reporters loved it, and after a while, I learned to laugh along with them—not because the memory was funny but because I was just grateful to still have all my limbs intact.

Speaking of press junkets, they're an experience unto themselves. Whenever a movie is about to be released, the publicists organize these events where actors (and sometimes directors) sit through interviews with a series of journalists, often in the same hotel room, one after the other. It's a bit like speed dating, except instead of awkward small talk, it's the same questions repeatedly.

I did my junket rounds for The Craze with Katherine Walls, who played my ex-wife in the movie. It was great having a partner to share the spotlight with, but the most challenging part of press junkets, and something I always tell my students, is coming up with fresh answers to the same questions. You're not supposed to lie; just change the wording enough to keep things interesting.

Even though I wasn't a fan of junkets, sitting there with the camera crews, answering questions from various reporters, was another reminder that I'd made it in the industry. I remember waiting for the next journalist to walk in, thinking about how far I'd come. I went from being homeless in L.A. to starring in a popular TV show and now a big studio movie.

"Why are you smiling?" Katherine asked, noticing the grin on my face.

"Just thinking," I replied, not even realizing I had been smiling.

Shortly after the junkets, I learned that the second season of *Country Doctors* would be filmed in Georgia, in a town called Ivywood.

"Where the fuck is Ivywood?" Laura asked when I told her. She wasn't mad—just her usual blunt self.

We had grown closer by the end of the summer. It was not in the whirlwind romance sense, but it was close enough that we decided to rent a house together while filming in Ivywood. I suppose, after working together so much, it made sense. We'd already spent a lot of time together, and sharing a house seemed more practical than being stuck in separate, dingy apartments.

Still, it wasn't a relationship born out of convenience. Our feelings had been there from the beginning, even during that first table read. But we'd waited, especially considering everything that had happened with Tina. We didn't rush into anything; by the time we ended up together, it felt right.

Moving to a place like Ivywood was a bit of a leap, especially since I'd only ever lived in Minnesota and Los Angeles. But Laura? She'd moved across continents, from

Australia to the U.S., so a small town in Georgia was nothing to her.

While it wasn't quite the glamorous jet-setting I'd imagined when I dreamed of being an actor, there was something exciting about relocating for a show. It was all part of the adventure. At least, that's what I thought.

I didn't know that this particular adventure would come to an unpleasant and unexpected halt.

15

Ivywood was the very definition of "quaint."

It had all the trappings of a small town but felt larger than most. The main street was lined with shops, a park, and a coffee house, with a small pond and a bronze horse statue gracing the park. I don't usually call towns beautiful, but Ivywood earned it.

Downtown, there was a boardwalk that hugged the edge of a large man-made lake. It was made of weathered wood, illuminated by old-fashioned lamps that lined the path. Those lights gave the town a calm, nostalgic feeling at night, which I appreciated after long days on set.

The Rising Star Studios location, near the outskirts of Ivywood, was surprisingly larger than its counterpart in Burbank. From our house, which was perched on a small hill near the man-made lake, you could spot the studios in the distance.

The house Laura and I bought was perfect for our time there. It was white, two stories, and had three bedrooms and three bathrooms—it wasn't some Malibu mansion, but it had a rustic charm. The previous owners had remodeled it with a lot of care. Everything looked antique, from the light fixtures to the hardwood floors, but our realtor assured us it was all newly installed.

The best part of the house? The patio. It didn't have a built-in grill or a bar area, but it offered something rare in L.A.: peace and quiet. Tall trees loomed over us like natural umbrellas, and the freshly stained wooden deck gleamed in the sunlight. I'd sit out there on particularly long days, letting the calm sink in.

For all the glitz and glamour people think comes with acting, most of it is anything but glamorous. Twelve-hour days, memorizing endless lines, dealing with demanding directors—it takes a toll. After a full day, you're grateful for a place like that patio or a quiet walk along Ivywood's boardwalk.

And yet, Ivywood itself was a pleasant surprise. Neither Laura nor I had been thrilled about moving to a small Georgia town, but the people more than made up for it. Southern hospitality is no myth. Folks in town greeted us with friendly conversation, not just because they recognized us but because that's who they were.

Even Craig—our resident grump—couldn't completely ignore the place's charm.

On set, I struck up a friendship with a P.A. named Montana, a guy from Billings who introduced himself with a laid-back "Just call me Montana." We'd hang out during downtime, playing cribbage in my trailer. He kicked my ass at it more often than not, but I taught him chess, and he taught me Spades. It was the perfect way to unwind between scenes.

Near the trailers was a tall, always-locked gate where young fans would gather, eager to catch a glimpse of us or score an autograph. Laura and I often stopped to sign things and take pictures, sliding autographs under the gap in the gate. On the other hand, Craig walked by them without so much as a glance.

One day, I asked him why he wouldn't interact with the fans. His response? "What if one of them pulls out a gun and blows your head off?"

It was a fair point, but I felt he didn't want to bother. We didn't let it stop us from greeting the fans—until the day it did.

Montana and I had just wrapped up a game of cribbage, and for once, I'd beaten him. We were heading to set for a scene where Danny tries to make up with Patty after cheating on her with her sister. It was one of my least favorite arcs in the show, especially since it also marked the start of Danny's verbal abuse toward Patty. I hated that storyline and thought it was unnecessary.

As we walked toward set, a crowd had gathered at the gate. Fans were shouting at me, clearly unhappy with Danny's actions on the show. The insults flew fast:

"What are you doing? Patty's a sweetheart!"
"Leave Patty alone, asshole!"
"Try that shit with me, tough guy!"
"Fuck you, Danny!"
"Have a drink!"

The last one barely registered before I felt a sharp, burning pain at the back of my head, followed by the sound of shattering glass. I turned around, and there on the dirt ground were the jagged remains of a broken beer bottle glistening in the sun. Blood trickled down my neck, soaking the collar of my shirt.

Montana was more pissed than I was. He called security while rushing me inside. The on-set medic cleaned the cut and patched me up, but I could hear the fans shouting more obscenities as we walked. It wasn't Danny they hated—it felt personal.

"Ethan!" Laura ran toward me, her face a mask of worry. "Oh my God, are you okay?"

"I'm fine," I reassured her, trying to sound calm. "Just a fan getting a little too enthusiastic."

"But... all that blood..." She stared at the back of my head, wide-eyed.

"Head wounds bleed a lot. It's the blood vessels up here," I said, trying to sound clinical despite the pain.

The medic confirmed I didn't need stitches, just a liquid bandage to seal the wound. By some miracle, we still filmed the scenes we had planned for that day. Nobody ever saw the cut on-screen, thanks to the bandage and makeup artists.

That incident made me realize how seriously some fans take their favorite shows and characters. Until then, nobody had ever treated me like I *was* the character I played, even back when I was Tommy Hughes on *Sealed Lips*. No one had ever hurled insults at me—or, God forbid, beer bottles.

When people ask if that moment made me uneasy, I always say it didn't affect me as much as when Tina was killed. But looking back, that was the first time I understood the dangerous side of fame.

It was a wake-up call.

But what happened next…

That was much worse.

16

Spring break for Alex in 2009 fell during the second full week of April.

That's when he and our mother flew down from Minnesota to surprise me. I hadn't seen either of them in a long time—Alex and I hadn't met face-to-face in a couple of years, and I hadn't seen my mother since leaving for college.

We talked on the phone and emailed often, but there's nothing like having your family there in person. You can smell their familiar scent—perfume, cologne, or even just their soap—and feel their arms around you in a hug. Those little things mean more than words can express.

It was a Saturday, and I had just gotten out of the shower when I saw Laura sitting on the edge of our bed, wearing a sly smile. It was the kind of smile a kid gives when they're about to spring a surprise.

"Wanna go to The Ivy Inn tonight?" she asked.

The Ivy Inn was a steakhouse in downtown Ivywood. We'd talked about going before but never found the time, which was odd because Laura and I loved steak. Laura was all about a good porterhouse while I leaned toward a New York strip.

We had no plans for the evening, so I shrugged and agreed. Once we arrived at the restaurant, I spotted Alex and our mother sitting in the lobby, grinning ear to ear. Laura laughed excitedly—clearly, she was in on the surprise.

Seeing them made me tear up a little. I hugged Alex first, thrilled to see him, but the real moment hit when I saw my mom's wide smile. She called my name softly before we embraced, and it was a long, warm hug—the kind that made me realize just how much I'd missed her.

"I've missed you so much!" she whispered. It wasn't meant for anyone else to hear, but it landed right where it was needed.

"I've missed you too, Mom," I whispered back.

I managed to keep it together, though I discreetly wiped a tear from my eye as we broke apart. It was just one of those moments, you know?

After our reunion, I introduced Laura to my family properly. Alex was excited to meet her—she was the first celebrity he'd ever met. On the other hand, my mom was calm and professional, though I suspected she was hiding a bit of star-struck excitement.

During dinner, Alex eagerly shared his plans for the future. He was gearing up to graduate high school in June and was waiting to hear back from colleges. His guidance counselor told him he had a good shot at getting into Berkeley's mechanical engineering program, which had him buzzing with excitement.

My mom, on the other hand, kept most of the conversation focused on me. When I asked her what was new, she casually mentioned treating a patient with rabies—a first in her 30-year medical career. I found it fascinating, but I didn't want to steer the conversation too far into medical territory since Alex was still discussing his plans.

When I asked about our father, Alex gave a quick answer, but my mother's reaction caught my attention. She hesitated, her expression shifting slightly before she replied, "He's good, just very busy with a case."

Something in her tone felt off, and she seemed more interested in cutting her grilled chicken than discussing my dad. I decided not to push the subject—at least, not with Alex there—but I filed the moment away, knowing I'd return to it later.

We shifted the conversation to lighter topics, and soon Laura chimed in with an idea: "Would you two be interested in working as extras on the show?"

Alex's eyes lit up, and my mom seemed intrigued by the suggestion. That week, we were filming a high school cafeteria scene where Danny and Patty reconciled, and we needed plenty of extras for the background.

Usually, people wanting to be extras had to apply at the casting office and wait for a call, but I told them to come with me to the set on Monday. Even if they couldn't work as extras, they could still watch us film and get a behind-the-scenes experience.

Unfortunately, things didn't quite go as planned. Alex and my mom couldn't work as extras until Wednesday, but the production team allowed them to sit behind the cameras on Monday to watch the filming.

They got to meet Patrick, who was often on set, and even Craig, who was surprisingly friendly. He shook Alex's hand, smiled at my mom, and said, "Nice to meet you. Hope you have a good time!" in his natural Australian accent—a sharp contrast to his Southern twang on the show.

I couldn't help but wonder what had caused Craig's sudden attitude shift. Usually, he barely made eye contact with people, but here he was, being all smiles. Whatever the reason, I wasn't going to complain. I wanted Alex and Mom's visit to the studio to be as positive as possible, and Craig playing nice helped.

That day, we filmed a scene where Danny begged Patty for forgiveness. It was a tough one—made even more difficult because her new boyfriend, Tyler (Craig's character), was hiding in her closet. An intense fight scene followed between Danny and Tyler, with lots of shouting and carefully choreographed moves.

Alex and my mom were amazed at how technical everything was. They couldn't stop talking about the fight choreography and how precise Craig and I had to be to avoid hurting each other.

Another thing they couldn't stop talking about? The lemonade from craft services. It was some of the best lemonade anyone had ever tasted—freshly squeezed, perfectly sweet and tart, with just the right amount of zing. We all had several cups, and I'm sure the craft team spent more time making lemonade than anything else.

As we left the studio that day, Alex asked, "What are you filming tomorrow?"

I told him we were doing the high school cafeteria scene, where both he and our mom would finally get to be extras. Alex would be one of the students at our table, while Mom would play a teacher on "lunchroom duty." We were all excited, especially Alex. It was the first time we'd work together on something like this.

That night, I checked the call sheet to ensure everything was set for the next day. It was all there—an early start at 7 a.m., Alex and Mom on the list of extras.

It was going to be a great day.

Or so I thought.

17

Today's the day, I thought, climbing out of bed.

I sat at the edge, glancing toward the closed bathroom door. Steam seeped from beneath it, accompanied by the muffled sound of running water. Laura had beaten me to the shower, and while I could've used the guest bathroom down the hall, that was currently Alex's and my mom's space. It didn't seem right to intrude.

While waiting for Laura, I checked the time on my phone—5:45 a.m. We had plenty of time. I leaned back against the headboard, scrolling through the morning's news. Some stories were important, others trivial. One headline stood out: *Ivywood Under Boil Water Advisory.*

An equipment failure at the water treatment plant had the town advising residents to boil tap water for at least a minute before consuming it. While the water wasn't confirmed to be contaminated, they were playing it safe.

When I finished reading, Laura emerged from the bathroom, wrapped in a towel. Despite the early hour and the fact that Alex and my mother were just down the hall, Laura had that playful glint in her eyes. She crawled onto the bed, her skin still warm from the shower, and kissed me softly. I could taste the mint from her toothpaste.

"You taste good," I said, pulling away momentarily and grinning.

She laughed. "Had to brush with bottled water. Did you see the boil advisory?"

"I did," I nodded, pulling her closer. "Thanks for saving me some."

We shared another kiss, and I felt her laugh when my hand brushed against her bare chest. But soon, the moment passed, and we both returned to our morning routine, mindful of our guests.

Alex and my mom had also heard about the Boil Water Advisory. My mom made sure Alex knew, especially since he had this weird habit of letting the shower water hit his face before spitting it out. There was no rhyme or reason to it—just something he did. As odd habits go, it wasn't the worst. It could've been worse, I thought.

When we arrived at the studio, tape covered the drinking fountains, and signs warned of potential water contamination. My mom and I shared a knowing look, silently appreciating the precaution. The risks of unclean water are no joke, and we both knew too well the kind of pathogens that can wreak havoc on the body.

Before long, it was time to shoot. Alex and my mom headed to the extras' holding room, where Montana and the other P.A.s instructed them to stay quiet when the cameras roll, pantomime their actions, and always follow the director's lead.

For those unfamiliar with pantomiming, it's acting without sound—moving your mouth and body as if talking, but in complete silence. It's a crucial part of being an extra and always feels strange until you get used to it.

We began shooting the cafeteria scene—a pivotal moment in which Danny, Patty, and Tyler reconcile amidst high school drama. I scanned the room, spotting my mom seated with the other adult extras at the far end. I knew Alex would be at our table, as I'd arranged with the producers.

Sure enough, there he was, sitting among the teen extras. I tapped him on the shoulder, and he spun around, grinning.

"Hey, man," he said, tapping me back.

I smiled, genuinely happy to have him on set with Susan and me. It felt good to share this part of my life with them.

Patrick, directing as always, called for everyone's attention, waving his arms dramatically. "Alright, everyone," he announced. "We're going to do a few takes. Listen closely to instructions. Remember, when I say 'rolling,' you need to pantomime and keep quiet."

The extras, including Alex and my mom, nodded in unison, ready for their moment. The cameras started rolling, and we jumped into the scene. Alex pantomimed with the other extras while Laura, Craig, and I delivered our lines. Take after take, we worked through different angles—wide shots, close-ups, and alternating between focused shots of each character.

During the breaks between takes, Alex and I chatted, with Laura occasionally joining us. Craig, on the other hand, pulled out a book from his prop backpack and buried himself in it, his earlier sociable mood seemingly evaporated. I'd gotten used to his sudden mood shifts by then, so I let it go.

After several hours of filming, we broke for lunch. The catering team had set up a taco bar, offering soft and hard shells, ground beef, or chicken, with all the fixings—cheese, lettuce, salsa, and more. The craft services team also kept the famous lemonade flowing, which, as always, was a huge hit.

Alex, my mom, Laura, and I sat together at lunch, enjoying the meal. Surprisingly, Craig was back to being sociable again, engaging in conversation. His unpredictable attitude remained a mystery to me, but at least he was pleasant. Maybe something about being around my mom brought out his good side.

Once lunch wrapped, we headed back to the set to film the next scene—Danny cutting in line to talk to Patty. Playing the student I cut in front of, Alex shot me a dirty look. He couldn't say anything—extras can't speak unless they have a SAG card—but the expression was spot on.

By the time we finished for the day, it was nearly seven. Twelve-hour days were common on set, and while they could be exhausting, they were part of the job. Alex and my mom seemed to enjoy the experience despite the long hours. My mom, who used to work grueling shifts at the hospital, seemed to gain a new appreciation for the work I did. I could see it in her eyes, a quiet respect that hadn't always been there.

"Will they need extras for the rest of the week?" Alex asked as we packed up.

I shook my head. "Unfortunately not. We're wrapping the episode in the next couple of days." He looked disappointed but ultimately understood.

On their last night in Ivywood, Laura and I took Alex and my mom to *The Greek Blossom*, the best restaurant in town. Their gyros were the stuff of legend, and even though I'd never been much for Greek food, this place had changed my mind.

We had a great meal, laughing and reminiscing about the week. It was the perfect end to their visit. But as always, the hardest part was saying goodbye.

At the airport the following day, I gave Alex a long hug. "Be good, buddy. Kick ass in college. Don't be a stranger."

"Love you," he said, his voice quiet but steady.

"Love you too."

Next, I hugged my mom. "I'm so proud of you, honey," she whispered. "Thanks for your hospitality."

"Of course, Mom. You're always welcome here." I kissed her cheek, and she smiled, her eyes glistening.

We said our goodbyes, and I watched them disappear into the airport. Once they were out of sight, I turned and headed home, already missing them.

18

The following Friday, I wasn't feeling well.

A lot of people weren't. Many wanted to call in sick, but we sucked it up like the rest of us. Montana was out, thinking he had a stomach bug.

I was feverish, running to the bathroom between takes like other actors, most notably Laura and Craig. Though none of us were throwing up—yet—we barely ate anything for breakfast, lunch, and dinner.

Tylenol was our saving grace. Our stomachs were twisted up, but at least the fevers broke long enough for us to make it through filming. As they say, the show must go on.

That night, back at home, Laura and I felt a little better. We managed to get down peanut butter and jelly sandwiches, thinking we were finally in the clear. A few hours later, we went to bed, grateful that our bout with whatever stomach bug we had was behind us.

But it wasn't over.

Just after two in the morning, I shot up in bed, my stomach twisting like someone was wringing it out. Despite the air conditioning, I was hot and sweaty.

"Laur," I started to say, but then I heard her.

From the bathroom, the sound of Laura groaning. It was the sound you make when someone tells you the worst dad joke ever.

The churn in my gut turned into an urgent push. I threw off the covers and bolted down the hall. Usually, I'd grab my slippers, but now wasn't the time to be a diva. I barely made it to the guest bathroom before I threw up, clenching my eyes shut to block out the sight of what was coming up.

The wave stopped as quickly as it had begun, and I blindly reached for the toilet handle to flush when—

Oh no.

A new urge hit me like a freight train. I barely had time to slam the seat down and drop my pajama bottoms before it started.

What was this? Food poisoning?

I had no idea, but the next day, I found Laura and me laid out on the sofa, groaning through stomach cramps and alternating trips to the bathroom. It was a full day of dry heaves and cramping, interrupted only by the occasional need for a peanut butter and jelly sandwich or toast.

That Saturday, we were lucky enough to be off from filming *Country Doctors*, but if it had been a workday, we would've been on set, feverish and miserable. Actors don't get sick days. Many times, I'd gone to work congested or running a fever, reciting my lines with a cold sweat clinging to my skin.

By Monday, the show was put on hold. Too many cast and crew members had fallen ill, some even in the hospital. The producers finally called for a temporary halt in filming.

What was going on?

At the end of the week, we got the answer. Several people had been diagnosed with E. coli O157, the pathogen that was found in the Ivywood Water Treatment Center on the day the Boil Water Advisory went out.

Suddenly, it all made sense.

How did we get it? Laura and I were so careful. We didn't drink the tap water, and we didn't brush our teeth with it. Then I remembered the lemonade.

I felt a chill crawl up my spine. Oh God. The lemonade. That meant everyone at the studio was exposed.

And Susan and Alex.

"Ethan!" Laura's voice snapped me out of my thoughts.

She stood in the bathroom doorway, her hand cradling her stomach.

"There's blood," she said, her eyes wide with panic.

My heart sank—bloody diarrhea. I knew what that meant.

"It's a common symptom," I said, trying to calm my voice. "We'll keep an eye on it."

Laura nodded, but I could see the fear in her eyes. I wasn't too worried yet. I knew what the symptoms meant and what to watch out for. E. coli infections usually clear up with rest and proper care.

But then my phone rang. I pulled it out of my pocket and stared at the screen.

It was Jeff. My father.

The panic hit me like a brick. Was it Susan and Alex?

"Hello?" I answered, my voice trembling.

"Ethan, it's your dad," Jeff said, his tone serious. "Susan and Alex are in the hospital."

I closed my eyes, my stomach twisting.

Alex had developed HUS—hemolytic uremic syndrome. My heart dropped. HUS was serious, affecting the kidneys and blood clotting. This wasn't just a bad case of the stomach flu anymore.

Jeff sent me photos of Susan and Alex in their hospital beds. Susan smiled weakly, but Alex was hooked up to tubes and machines.

"Sorry I didn't call sooner," Jeff said.

I couldn't even respond. There was nothing to say.

19

It had been years since Laura and I had flown coach.

Neither of us could even remember the last time we flew first class, but that was only because flying first class had become commonplace whenever we flew. Because it was last minute, coach was all that was available.

We were crammed into narrow seats with little legroom, scripts for the next episode of *Country Doctors* spread out on our tray tables. After returning from Minneapolis, we'd start filming again the following Monday.

I had been a wreck since hearing the news about Susan and Alex. Every time I saw a mother with her children or what I imagined to be two brothers, my eyes would well up. The only thing that kept me from breaking down was taking a deep breath and pressing my lips together until the urge passed.

It felt like a bad dream. Susan passed away in the morning, and Alex that night. I lost two people I loved on the same day. Later, I learned that Susan died from complications of severe dehydration, while Alex's organs failed because of HUS. I prayed neither of them had suffered.

When our plane landed, we deboarded, and I found myself aching from the cramped seat and lack of legroom. I scolded myself for even noticing—my family had died, and here I was, fretting about my legs.

Laura didn't say anything about her discomfort, but I could tell her legs were sore by the way she shuffled through the terminal. Still, we stopped for autographs and a few quick photos with fans as we made our way to baggage claim.

Once we retrieved our bags, which seemed to take forever, we rented a car and drove to our hotel in downtown Minneapolis. It was a nice hotel, but nothing luxurious.

Laura glanced at me while waiting in the long line to check-in. "Why can't we just stay with your dad?"

I ignored the question. Normally, I'd consider that rude, but I made an exception this time. It was a fair question. After all, Jeff had called to tell me about Susan and Alex. But that was it—he hadn't offered anything more, not even condolences. The last words he said before hanging up were, "You should come to the funeral."

"I mean, you'd think he'd bury the hatchet after what happened," Laura said softly.

She had a point. I gave a slight shrug and nodded, acknowledging the truth in her words. My mind wandered to the double funeral that would take place in a couple of days. How would it feel to see Jeff after all these years? Susan had forgiven me, but Jeff? That was a whole other story.

In my heart, I knew Jeff's call was more out of obligation than anything else. The tone in his voice had been so cold, detached—as though he was calling a distant acquaintance, not his son. I had wondered if he even wanted me to come at all.

The wake is tomorrow. I'll see him tomorrow, I thought, feeling a knot of anxiety tighten in my chest.

Laura nudged me back to reality. "We're next," she whispered, guiding me to the front desk.

Our room had a king bed, a large bathroom, and a beautiful view of the Mississippi River. In the distance, if you squinted, you could see the Stone Arch Bridge. It was a great room, though I found it hard to appreciate given the circumstances.

We dropped our bags and decided to go for a walk, hoping some fresh air would clear our heads. Minneapolis was cold, though spring was on its way, and most of the snow had melted. As we walked, we noticed that the locals were only wearing light jackets, while Laura and I were bundled in parkas, still unaccustomed to the chill of Minnesota after living in Southern California for so long.

We found a small Mexican restaurant for dinner, and as we ate, Laura asked me about my early days in L.A. I told her the story about my first meal at a Mexican restaurant and the awkward job offer I'd gotten to work as an escort. She laughed, as she always did whenever I told that story, though she never let me live it down.

Then I asked about her story.

Laura hesitated for a moment, then started talking about her journey from Australia to L.A., the struggles of breaking into acting, and how she'd started in theater.

But when she mentioned a certain director she'd worked with, her hands trembled. She tried to cover it up by taking a sip of water, but I knew her well enough.

"Are you okay?" I asked gently.

She nodded, but her face faltered when I asked how she'd enjoyed working with him. Then, in a quiet voice, she told me how that director had lured her into a private room under the guise of discussing her role—and sexually assaulted her.

My heart sank. I slid out of my seat and into hers, wrapping my arms around her as she cried softly into my chest. Our server approached, but I waved them away, mouthing, "We're okay."

After paying the bill, we took a cab back to the hotel, Laura still trembling slightly. Back in our room, we lay on the bed, curled up together—not for romance, but for comfort. She needed it, and so did I.

The next day, Laura and I arrived early at Augusta Funeral Home for Susan's and Alex's wake. The room was packed—friends and co-workers of Jeff and Susan, along with Alex's friends and his girlfriend, Penny.

People recognized Laura and me, but no one asked for autographs or photos. This wasn't the time or place. We were all there to mourn.

When I saw Susan and Alex in their caskets, it hit me. This was real. They were really gone. Susan, dressed in her favorite purple dress, looked peaceful as if she were sleeping. Alex, in his suit and tie, looked as sharp as ever. But the stillness, the cold reality of their deaths, was undeniable.

Throughout the wake, Jeff and I didn't speak. He had shaken my hand when Laura and I arrived, offering a curt "Good to see you," but that was the extent of our interaction. His smile was fake, the kind you'd give to someone you barely tolerate.

I thought maybe the deaths of his wife and son would make him want to move past the old grudge. But I was wrong. Seeing the same coldness in his eyes as when I had first left for L.A., I realized Jeff had probably never forgiven me. Not fully.

Toward the end of the wake, Penny stood up and read a poem she had written for Alex. Her voice cracked as she looked over at his casket, tears streaming down her face. A friend rushed to her side, escorting her back to her seat.

It was a poignant way to end the wake and a tough day for everyone. But I had a feeling tomorrow—the funeral—would be even harder.

20

The day of Susan's and Alex's funeral was, by far, the worst.

Jeff gave me a nod of acknowledgment—nothing more. I watched as he shook hands with his co-workers, hugged other family members, and offered warmth to everyone but me. It felt like a hot, dull knife was being driven into my stomach, the pain slow and deliberate. At the wake, he had at least exchanged a few empty words with me, but here, at their funeral, it was as if I didn't even exist.

"He probably has his own way of dealing with grief," Laura whispered, her hand resting on my thigh as we sat in the pews. She was trying to comfort me and rationalize his behavior, but it only made me angrier.

"Then why is he talking to everyone else but me?" I asked quietly, though it wasn't really a question. It was more of a bitter observation, and I didn't expect her to answer.

Laura shrugged, giving me a small smile as if to say, *I don't know either.* But that didn't stop the knot in my chest from tightening as I stared ahead at the two caskets in front of the altar.

Susan and Alex. My mother. My little brother.

I couldn't bring myself to walk up to their caskets again. Everyone else had gone up—Jeff, other relatives, friends—but not me. I'd seen them the day before at the wake, and that had been painful enough. Today, it felt unbearable. The finality of their deaths weighed heavily on my shoulders, pressing down with a kind of force that made my legs feel like lead.

I sat there, gripping Laura's hand a little too tightly, trying to keep my emotions in check. Some part of me—the irrational, grief-stricken part—half-expected them to sit up in their caskets, laughing and telling us this was all some kind of sick prank. Maybe Jeff would even come over and give me a hug, his icy demeanor melting away in the face of a bizarre family joke. But that was just a fantasy, a desperate wish in the middle of an impossible reality.

Susan and Alex weren't getting up. And Jeff wasn't going to embrace me.

The service ended at the cemetery, where they would soon be buried. I stood by their gravestones, staring at the freshly dug earth, trying to make sense of it all. The cold air bit at my skin, though not as harshly as when Laura and I first arrived. Still, we zipped our leather jackets up to our chins, hands shoved deep into our pockets as we tried to stave off the chill.

The sky was overcast, clouds shrouding the sun with only occasional glimpses of light breaking through. I wanted to get out of there before the gravediggers started their work. Something about the idea of watching Susan and Alex lowered into the ground felt too final, too real.

"Ethan," a voice said from behind me.

I turned to see Jeff approaching, his face unreadable but somehow heavier than before. I felt a jolt of unease in my chest as he came closer. I hadn't expected him to talk to me, not after the way he'd ignored me throughout the funeral.

"I'm glad you could come," he said, his tone flat.

"Why wouldn't I?" I replied, my voice tinged with bitterness. "My mother and little brother just died."

He ignored my comment and turned to Laura. "You must be Laura Preston. Alex and Susan spoke very highly of you."

He extended his hand, and Laura hesitated for just a moment before taking it. Jeff didn't smile—not even a polite one. His face remained solemn, distant, as though Laura were just another person to cross off the list of social pleasantries.

Laura managed a small smile in return but said nothing. Jeff turned back to me.

"So," he began, his voice slightly louder as he enunciated each syllable with forced precision, "how are things in... *Hollywood*?" The way he said it, emphasizing "Hollywood," made it clear that this wasn't a simple question. It was a challenge, laced with all the anger and resentment he had bottled up for years.

I sighed. "Dad, I don't want to argue. This isn't the time or the place."

"This is the perfect time," he said, his voice dripping with sarcasm as he gave me a mocking thumbs-up, clearly referencing one of my old modeling ads. It was a black-and-white photo of me emerging from the ocean in a swimsuit, with the tagline: *This is Ethan Mitchell. He is Perfection. You can be Perfection, too.*

I clenched my jaw, my patience wearing thin. But before I could say anything, Laura stepped forward. "Excuse me," she said politely, "but I don't think this is the appropriate time or place for this."

Jeff turned to her, his eyes narrowing. "This doesn't concern you, Ms. Preston," he said coldly.

His tone was like a slap in the face, and Laura recoiled slightly, her gaze dropping to the ground. I felt a surge of anger rise in my chest.

"You know, Dad," I began, my voice low but steady, "you're not the only one who lost loved ones today. So I would appreciate it if you didn't take it out on my girlfriend."

Jeff turned back to me, his expression hardening. "This is between you and me, Ethan. It has nothing to do with her."

I took a deep breath, my hands balling into fists inside my jacket pockets. "Can't you just find a way to forgive me? Mom did."

He shook his head, his cold facade cracking just enough to reveal a flicker of sadness. "That's because your mother had a heart of gold. She was always too forgiving."

"And you're really still this mad at me?" I asked, incredulous.

"You have no idea," he said, his voice low and shaking. "You have no idea how a parent feels when their child suddenly decides to drop out of college and move across the country to chase a dream in one of the hardest industries to break into. I was terrified. There were nights I didn't sleep at all. I had to see a psychiatrist, Ethan, because it was killing me inside."

I stared at him, my anger evaporating, replaced by guilt. "I'm sorry, Dad. I'm really, really sorry. I didn't know it hurt you like that."

"It's a little late for apologies," he said, his voice thick with emotion. "Maybe... maybe one day I'll forgive you. But today is not that day."

With that, he turned and walked away, leaving me standing there, speechless. He didn't even glance back.

I stood frozen for a moment, trying to process everything that had just happened. The weight of it all—the funeral, the confrontation, the unresolved tension—made me feel like I was suffocating.

"That was worse than the wake," I muttered, my voice hollow.

Laura slipped her hand into mine, squeezing gently. "Let's just go back to the hotel," she said softly. "We don't need to stay here any longer."

I nodded. I didn't have the strength to argue.

When we got back to the hotel, we changed out of our funeral clothes and spent the rest of the day in bed, watching TV in silence. Neither of us felt like talking. We ordered room service for lunch and dinner, barely touching our food.

The next day, we'd be on a plane back to Ivywood.

And the day after that, we'd be back on set, pretending everything was normal.

21

Upon our return to Ivywood, Rising Star Studios was as busy as ever.

Despite the usual hustle and chaos, an odd calm seemed to blanket the buildings like an invisible fog. P.A.s dashed around fetching coffee for the director, but even their hurried movements appeared sluggish as if the urgency had been sucked out of the day. Voices rose to give orders, yet everything sounded muted like someone had turned the volume down on the world.

The vibe in the studio mirrored my state of mind. Concentration, which had always been a strength, was slipping through my fingers. I flubbed my lines, missed my marks, and delivered performances so stiff I felt embarrassed to watch the playbacks. If I were the director, I would've fired me on the spot.

Patrick, who was directing that day, approached after yet another ruined take. "Look, Ethan, you've gotta get your head in the game. I know you've been through a lot, but I need you to focus," he said, sounding more like a coach than a director.

I nodded, apologizing, but the truth was I didn't know how to fix it. The deaths of Susan and Alex hung over me like a dark cloud, and no matter how hard I tried, I couldn't shake it. During lunch, I locked myself in my trailer, trying to focus, trying to snap out of it. Laura and Craig stopped by to help me run lines, their support like lifelines pulling me out of the fog.

It was strange how people had changed since I returned to set. Craig, who had always been distant and aloof, was suddenly compassionate. He had been the first to greet me that morning, walking up without a word and pulling me into a hug. "If you need to talk, let me know," he had said, his voice soft but sincere. I wasn't used to seeing this side of him.

Montana had changed, too, though in a different way. He had always been friendly and quick to chat during downtime. Now, he was all business. He barely said anything beyond what was necessary for work, his usual warmth replaced with a cool professionalism. It was like a switch had flipped, and I couldn't help but wonder if my grief had somehow made him uncomfortable. Maybe he didn't know how to handle it, so he distanced himself.

By the end of the day, after running lines with Laura and Craig and giving myself a pep talk in the trailer bathroom, I managed to get through the remaining scenes without too many mistakes. As the days passed, I began to slip back into the rhythm of filming—reciting lines, hitting marks, delivering performances that felt closer to what I used to do before everything fell apart.

But something was off, and I wasn't the only one who noticed. Fans of *Country Doctors*, along with the media, began to pick apart the show. The storylines were weaker, sure, but that wasn't what hurt the most. It was the criticism of my performances. Laura, Craig, and the rest of the cast were praised, but my work was relentlessly torn apart. People speculated that I had turned to drugs to cope with my family's deaths, and the accusations cut deeper than any review of my acting ever had.

One critic wrote in his blog, *"Ethan Mitchell's performance in last night's episode was like watching a first-grader attempt Shakespeare. It was terrible! Let's hope no other actors lose family members, or we'll be stuck with performances like this all season."*

It was vicious, and it felt personal. When Kevin heard about it, he was furious. He wanted me to sue the critic or, at the very least, call for his resignation. But I couldn't. The critic hadn't attacked my family—he was attacking my acting. As brutal as his words were, they were within his rights. I wasn't about to stir up more drama by filing a lawsuit over something as subjective as a performance review. Besides, the critic ran his own blog, so it wouldn't have changed anything even if I could have gotten him fired. Kevin didn't understand and kept pushing until I finally told him to back off politely.

But the damage had been done. The longer I stayed on set, the more disinterested I became. My heart just wasn't in it anymore. Laura noticed before I even said a word. One night, after a particularly rough day, she suggested I take a break from acting—just a brief sabbatical once we wrapped for the season.

It sounded perfect. After all, we'd be done filming in April or May, and the following season wouldn't start until late August. I figured a few months away from the cameras might be exactly what I needed to reset.

If, of course, there even *was* a next season. Ratings were in freefall, and Craig had already told his agent to start looking for new projects. It felt like we were all waiting for the inevitable.

Sure enough, the network didn't renew us for a sixth season. The series finale of *Country Doctors* aired, leaving fans outraged by its ambiguous ending. In case you missed it, my character, Danny, was diagnosed with mesothelioma after helping his grandfather remove old insulation from a storage shed. The final scene was Patty receiving a phone call from the hospital, her face crumpling in horror. Just as her mother asked what was wrong, the screen cut to black, and the "Executive Producers" credit rolled.

It was the number one question fans asked me at conventions and meet-and-greets: *Did Danny die?* Honestly, I didn't know. I liked to think his cancer went into remission, but that was just my way of giving fans a little closure. The truth was, the writers hadn't given me an answer either.

After filming wrapped, we had a modest wrap party at Patrick's rented house on the outskirts of Ivywood. It wasn't anything fancy—a simple ranch-style house that lacked the glitz and glamor people usually associate with Hollywood. It was a bittersweet evening. We laughed and reminisced, and for a few hours, it almost felt like the old days.

Later, Laura, Craig, and I walked through downtown Ivywood, soaking in the rustic charm of the place. The town had been our home for so long, and the realization that this chapter was closing hit harder than expected. Laura started crying as we wandered along the boardwalk, the soft glow of the lights reflecting off the lake's still waters. I wrapped my arm around her, holding her close as she quietly sobbed into my shoulder.

"This was my first time in the country," Craig suddenly said, staring at the water.

I glanced at him, surprised. "Really?"

He nodded, his gaze distant. "Yeah. I've never even been on a farm."

His words caught me off guard. Craig, the city boy who had always seemed so at ease in any setting, suddenly admitted that this rural world had been entirely foreign to him.

"That's why I wanted to become an actor," he continued. "I wanted to escape the city... to see something new, something different."

There was a vulnerability in his voice that I hadn't heard before. He wasn't just talking about travel—he was talking about breaking free from something deeper, something that had been suffocating him for years.

I didn't press him for more. Instead, I just nodded, understanding in my own way. Acting was an escape for all of us in one way or another, but Craig had never let on how much he needed it until that night.

Little did I know, *Country Doctors* would be the last starring role I'd ever have.

22

After *Country Doctors* ended, the quality of the scripts being sent to me plummeted.

Some of the material was so bad that even the script I wrote as a kid for *The Action Figure* seemed better. No exaggeration.

Being back in L.A. required some adjustment after spending most of the last five years in Ivywood. When I did fly back to L.A. during those years, it was always for short stints. Back when I could only dream of becoming an actor, I imagined how cool it would be to travel to different places, not for a vacation, but to shoot projects. I tell my students that while it might seem glamorous, the constant travel eventually wears you down.

Some actors might disagree. Sure, going to Paris for a film shoot sounds like a dream, and you could sightsee on your days off. But after weeks or months of being there, the novelty wears off, and all you want to do is go home. It could be Paris, London, or New York City—anywhere. And it's worse when you're shooting a TV series because you're in the same place for much longer.

Don't get me wrong, Ivywood was a great town. But after five years, I was ready to come home. Settling back into L.A. felt good. After selling our house in Ivywood, Laura and I bought a place on the Malibu coast. It had floor-to-ceiling windows in the sunroom, five bedrooms, six bathrooms, a basement with a bar, game room, gym, sauna, and a patio with a pool and hot tub.

The view of the ocean was sparse—you could only catch glimpses of it between the tall palm trees growing along the property. But we weren't complaining. The house cost over three million dollars, and living in it made us feel like true Hollywood celebrities. Sometimes, I'd stand there, thinking, *I came from washing dishes at a hotel, and now look at me.*

Thinking of the hotel reminded me of Luke. He'd been there from the beginning when my acting career was just a dream. I hadn't seen him in a while, so I decided to pay him a visit. The drive from Malibu to *The Oracle* in Beverly Hills was a little over half an hour—not too bad, even with L.A. traffic. Besides, I was Luke's business partner now, and I wasn't about to let a little traffic get in the way.

When I arrived, Luke was dealing with a situation at the front desk. A couple loudly complained about their honeymoon suite, drawing attention from everyone in the lobby. Even the guests at the bar had stopped sipping their cocktails to watch the show. Luke kept his cool, eventually having the unruly couple escorted out by security.

As soon as that fiasco ended, Luke spotted me. He came over and hugged me, his usual easygoing smile replaced by a somber expression. "I'm so sorry about Susan and Alex," he said, his voice low. It hit me hard—he was the first person outside my immediate circle who had brought up their deaths. His hug was strong and warm, and I could feel the emotions bubbling up inside me. Sensing this, Luke quickly suggested we head to his office.

Inside, he handed me a beer from his mini fridge, joking, "Sorry, I save the Dom Perignon for the guests." I smiled, grateful for the humor, and took a big swig.

We caught up for a bit. Luke told me that business at the hotel was booming and that he and Amanda were expecting their second child. They were planning a trip to Rome next month. He seemed genuinely happy. When it was my turn, I told him about my acting sabbatical and the new house. I mentioned my mixed feelings after *Country Doctors* ended and my time filming in Georgia. But when I said I was taking a break from acting, I noticed Luke's expression shift—he looked concerned.

An awkward silence filled the room. I took another drink of beer and asked, "What's on your mind?"

Luke leaned forward, resting his arms on his desk. "I just remember how passionate you were when you first moved out here," he said. "You were all in. From the day we met, all you talked about was acting."

I shrugged. "Yeah, I don't know. It's complicated."

He raised an eyebrow. "Are you sure this is just a sabbatical, or are you thinking of stepping back from acting for good?"

A year ago, I would've responded with a firm, "Absolutely not." But now, I wasn't so sure. I couldn't find the words, so I just shook my head.

Luke pressed on, his voice softer. "You don't seem to have the same spark you used to have. What changed?"

That was the question, wasn't it? What had changed? I'd achieved everything I set out to do—from being a hotel dishwasher to a celebrity. I'd experienced the highs of stardom. But maybe that was part of the problem. Once you've reached the peak, where do you go from there?

"I guess I just... don't feel the same way about it anymore," I admitted. "It's like a kid losing interest in a toy he once loved."

Luke nodded but didn't push further. He could see I didn't have all the answers yet.

Eventually, I ended the sabbatical because bills needed to be paid. I didn't want to start dipping into savings, so I called Kevin and told him to start finding me acting jobs again. Kevin had been annoyed when I first told him about the sabbatical. You could hear the irritation in his voice, the little pauses where he was trying to hold back. It made sense—this is how agents make their money. And while I wasn't his only client, I was one of his highest earners (not to brag). He was overjoyed when I told him I was ready to work again.

"I want smaller roles, no starring gigs," I reminded him.

"Gotcha, my man!" Kevin always called me "my man" or "sir." After a while, I wondered if he remembered my name.

While Kevin hunted for roles, I spent more time at *The Oracle*, shadowing Luke to see how the hotel ran. Not because I was interested in managing a hotel—far from it—but because it was my investment. I figured I should at least know the basics if something happened and Luke needed to step away. Not that I was expecting to take over anytime soon, thank God. Luke had a great assistant manager who could handle things if needed.

Eventually, Kevin found me some guest-starring roles on a few TV shows—one-episode gigs. For the first time, though, acting started to feel like a 9-to-5 job instead of the dream I once had. I mentioned it to Laura one night, and she shrugged it off.

"Don't worry about it," she said. "It happens. The same thing happened to me after a few years of acting. You get burned out, but it doesn't last forever."

Her words reassured me, though they didn't reignite the fire I once had. But they did remind me that I was still lucky. Countless actors in L.A.'d been at it for years and never booked a single gig. At least I was working. Still, the passion wasn't there, and I couldn't figure out why.

Then came *The Ballad of Airborne Ace*. It was a stage production, my first since high school. I played Xavier Ward, a college basketball player who loses his scholarship due to heavy drinking and discovers a hidden talent for writing poetry. The role wasn't anything spectacular—certainly not Broadway material—but it was fun. And something about being on stage, in front of a live audience, brought back a little of the old spark.

It wasn't just the character or the story. It was the immediacy of theater, the connection with the audience, and the thrill of performing without the safety net of reshoots or editing. For the first time in a while, I felt like I was doing what I was meant to do.

It wasn't enough to make me move to New York or pursue Broadway roles, but it was enough to remind me why I fell in love with acting in the first place.

L.A. was my home. It was where I belonged, at least for now.

23

Our house sat near a beautiful walking trail, but the only downside was that it could get busy, especially on the weekends.

Most of the time, people were walking, jogging, or cycling. I'd jog it regularly, and on a Saturday morning in October 2011, that's exactly what I was doing. I never bothered with a gym membership—Laura and I had a couple of exercise machines in a large storage room and, of course, our swimming pool.

And let's not forget that walking trail.

Contrary to popular belief, you don't need to be a chiseled, young, or tan actor to make it in Hollywood. Whether you're young, old, overweight, skinny, pale, or dark-skinned—it doesn't matter. Talent is what gets you hired. At least, eventually. Keeping up appearances is a lot less critical than people think, especially if you can comfortably afford the lifestyle. Some folks in these expensive neighborhoods might disagree, but it's not like you need a Rolls Royce or millions in the bank to live here.

That said, even our pricey neighborhood had its flaws. That morning, while jogging, I tripped over a crack in the pavement and took a spill. Other than a skinned knee, I was fine, but the blood dripping down my leg forced me to cut my run short. I hurried home, washed the wound, sprayed some disinfectant on it, and wrapped it up with gauze.

Just as I finished, my phone rang. It was Kevin.

"Hey, Ethan, my man! Did I wake you?" he asked, his voice chipper as usual.

I yawned, rubbing my eyes. "No, you're good. What's going on?"

"You'll never believe this. Patrick Schwartz is directing a movie based on the E. coli outbreak in Ivywood, and he wants you to invest."

I blinked, not sure I heard him right. Patrick? Making a movie about *that*? Sure, it was national news for a while, but did it need to be immortalized in a film? More importantly, did *I* want to get involved?

"No thanks, Kevin," I said, feeling a strange knot in my stomach. I hadn't expected to react so strongly, but the memories of that time were still raw. "I don't think I want to touch that one."

Kevin's upbeat tone faltered. "Too many painful memories?"

"Yeah, something like that."

Kevin paused, then asked gently, "You doing okay, man?"

"I'm fine," I assured him, though the truth was more complicated. "By the way, do you know if Craig or anyone else from *Country Doctors* is involved?"

Kevin didn't know but offered to find out. "No, it's fine. I was just curious," I said.

After exchanging the usual pleasantries, Kevin mentioned signing a new client, Liam Martinez. He was a young actor from Texas, and Kevin was pretty excited about him. I hadn't heard of the guy but wished Kevin the best.

Later, I brought up Patrick's new project with Laura. She hadn't heard about it, and her face mirrored my confusion. I texted Craig out of curiosity, and his reply came back quickly: *Yeah, I knew about it, but I'm not getting involved.* He was in Toronto working on a TV movie and seemed as uninterested in *The Plague* as I was.

The strange part was why Patrick had only asked us to invest and hadn't mentioned anything about consulting or participating further. I shot Craig another text, and he agreed it was odd. "I mean, we were *there*," Craig wrote, "Wouldn't you think he'd want some firsthand input?"

Even more curious, Patrick hadn't allowed us to see the script. I knew screenwriters could be secretive, but this was out of character for Patrick, who'd always been eager to share his work, no matter how polished—or how bad—it was. He was the type to hand out drafts, even letting us read his ridiculous stress-relief poetry. But with *The Plague*, he was locking it down. The secrecy was unnerving, and it only made me wonder more.

One night, Laura and I were flipping between channels, alternating between watching TV and sneaking in a few kisses, when we saw some coverage of *The Plague*. They had started filming in Wilmington, North Carolina. I hadn't known they were that far along. The city looked eerily similar to Ivywood.

What caught our attention wasn't just the location but the casting. Nathan Carter was playing me, Danielle Simmons was cast as Laura, Victoria Bell was playing Susan, and, to my surprise, Kevin's new client, Liam Martinez, was playing Craig.

I didn't mind Nathan as my stand-in; he was a solid actor, having starred in some popular teen dramas and a Civil War film. On the other hand, Laura was visibly annoyed at being portrayed by Danielle Simmons, a beauty influencer who occasionally popped up in online shorts. She made a face and muttered something about Simmons' lack of acting chops.

"She's not even an actress!" Laura scoffed. "They really cast her as me?"

I chuckled. "Maybe they think you're more glamorous than you let on."

Laura rolled her eyes, still fuming.

Victoria Bell playing my mom was a funny coincidence—she and I had both appeared on *Country Doctors* and *Sealed Lips* but never in the same scenes. And, of course, there was the little tidbit that Victoria had started her career in 70s porn. I couldn't help but find that amusing.

But what gnawed at me was who they cast as Alex. I asked Kevin if he could get any info from Liam, but due to contractual obligations, Liam couldn't spill anything. I understood, but it only fueled my curiosity.

And then there was that comment from Nathan Carter during an interview that made the hair on the back of my neck stand up. When asked what audiences could expect from *The Plague*, Nathan grinned slyly and said, "Just get ready for a hell of a scary thrill ride."

Thrill ride? A movie about an E. coli outbreak, a "thrill ride"? None of it made sense. How did a tragic health crisis become something thrilling or scary?

Laura and I looked at each other, confused, as the segment continued. The marketing team was clearly doing a great job keeping the plot under wraps, but it left a bitter taste in my mouth. How could they spin that horrible time into something... sensationalized?

"I don't get it," I muttered. "How is a story about E. coli a *thrill ride*?"

Laura shrugged, but I could see she was just as baffled. And maybe even a little hurt. We lived through that outbreak. I lost my mom and brother to it. The fact that Patrick had turned it into some horror thriller was starting to piss me off.

And it wasn't just me. Craig texted me later, "Man, what the hell is Patrick doing? He's gone full zombie flick with this."

Zombie flick? I stared at the text, my mind racing. How could Patrick take something so personal, something so devastating, and twist it into... this?

The more I thought about it, the angrier I got. This wasn't just a movie. It was a distortion of the worst time of my life. And Patrick, of all people, knew what that time had cost me. The secrecy, the misleading marketing, the casting—it all made me feel like the truth was being buried under a flashy Hollywood spectacle.

And it wasn't just disappointing. It was infuriating.

Big time.

24

June 2, 2012, was one of the most memorable days of my life.

Laura and I were married at St. Paul's Cathedral, just north of L.A. She wore a dress that seemed to have been made just for her—a perfect match for her grace and beauty. Watching her walk down the aisle, I could hardly believe that someone so incredible would choose to spend the rest of her life with me.

Her sister, Audrey, served as her Maid of Honor, and the rest of her family flew in from Melbourne. I hadn't anticipated how big her family was—good thing we split the costs! No, really, the whole wedding felt like something out of a dream, and not just because of the stunning dress or the grandeur of the cathedral.

I decided not to wear the same tuxedo I always donned for premieres or black-tie events. Instead, I rented one that, while simple, got me more compliments than I expected. Maybe people just weren't used to seeing me in anything different.

Craig was my Best Man. Considering how we'd gone from on-set enemies to genuine friends, it was fitting that he stood by my side. Along with Kevin and his girlfriend, who was also my new publicist, a few close friends attended on my side, including Luke, who was the first to RSVP. Of course, I sent an invitation to Jeff, my father, but I knew in my heart he wouldn't come.

His absence hurt more than I cared to admit. I was used to it by now, but that didn't make it any easier. At my wedding—the day that was supposed to be one of the happiest of my life—it still nagged at me that my own father couldn't bring himself to be there.

The reception was held at *The Oracle*, courtesy of Luke. His wedding gift to us, along with some kitchen gadgets, was the free use of the hotel's best banquet room. It was the same one where Luke had his stakeholders' party the night Tina died. A strange coincidence, but it didn't overshadow the joy of the day.

Despite the fun, laughter, and love all around, I couldn't entirely shake the thought of Jeff not showing up. It burrowed deep, like a thorn under my skin. I plastered on a smile, like I always did for cameras and events I wasn't keen on attending, but this was different. This wasn't just another public appearance—it was my wedding.

When it came time for our first dance, I confided in Laura about Jeff's absence. Her response was perfect, just like her.

"He might not be here, Ethan, but take a look at who *is* here," she said, placing her hand gently on my cheek and turning my head toward our guests. The smiles of our friends and family were warm and supportive.

Laura always knew how to pull me back from the edge. She made me focus on the good, reminding me why I loved her so much. At that moment, I realized just how lucky I was to have her by my side. She didn't care about her own happiness as much as mine, and that selflessness was one of the many reasons I had married her.

Our honeymoon in Moscow was a dream. We visited Red Square, saw a ballet at the Bolshoi Theatre, toured museums, and indulged in delicious Russian cuisine. Those two weeks flew by, but they were some of the best days of my life.

Upon returning to L.A., mixed in with our pile of mail was a large envelope addressed to both of us. Inside was an invitation to the premiere of *The Plague*. At first, it seemed like a typical movie premiere invite. Laura and I thought it would be just another horror-thriller, maybe with zombies or something equally absurd. Then, we remembered that actors were playing *us*.

It hit us with a jolt—we hadn't fully connected the dots. This movie wasn't just "inspired by" the Ivywood outbreak. It was about *us* and the events we lived through. The realization sank in, bringing with it a wave of unease. *The Plague* wasn't just a film—it was a version of our lives twisted for Hollywood.

Craig was also invited, and like us, he wasn't sure what to expect. I couldn't shake the worry, though. The thought of seeing Susan and Alex portrayed on screen kept gnawing at me. I had one desperate hope: *Be respectful to Susan and Alex.*

That phrase became a mantra in my head for the next month and a half. It crept into everything I did, even while memorizing lines for a guest spot on a TV show. No matter how hard I tried to focus, the anxiety seeped in.

It only got worse when Patrick called me out of the blue a few weeks before the premiere.

"Hey, Ethan! Excited about the premiere?" he asked, sounding cheerful.

"I guess," I replied, but then quickly asked, "How are my mother and brother portrayed in this movie?"

There was a long pause on the other end of the line. Too long. Finally, Patrick said, "The actors playing them do a respectable job."

That did nothing to ease my fears. It was the kind of answer someone gives when dodging the real issue. I wanted to press him but knew it wouldn't get me anywhere. Patrick wasn't going to tell me what I needed to know.

Before we hung up, he asked how the wedding and honeymoon had gone, but it felt like an afterthought. His voice lacked the usual warmth, as if he was trying to fill the silence. I couldn't help but feel uneasy after the call, a sensation that stayed with me until the day of the premiere.

When August 31 finally arrived, Laura wore a stunning blue satin backless dress, her pearls gleaming in the lights. She looked like a movie star—graceful, poised, beautiful. I wore a black button-up shirt with white dress pants, a contrast to her elegance but fitting for the event.

Walking the red carpet was magical. Laura and I held hands, stopping for photographers and answering questions from journalists. They all wanted to know the same thing—whether we knew what the movie was about and whether we were excited. We answered in sync, like a well-rehearsed duo, and it felt like we were in this together, facing whatever the night had in store.

But the red carpet was the only magical part of the evening.

The movie itself? Well, that was something else entirely.

25

"Oh my God. What a piece of shit."

Those words were whispered by Laura about halfway through *The Plague*. I think she was just being polite.

While I won't waste your time with a complete plot summary, especially if you've already seen it, I will tell you this: the film was a mockery. Not only did it piss me off, but it angered many of the real people who were used as characters.

Patrick made me look like an arrogant douchebag, Laura like a talentless, sex-crazed slut, and my mother like a stuck-up witch. And Alex? My brother only existed when it was convenient—not for the story, but for shock value. I'll get to that.

If you haven't seen *The Plague* and plan to, I'm sorry for these spoilers. But honestly, you'll be better off knowing.

In the movie, "Laura" has an affair with "Patrick." They sneak into his trailer when she's infected but not yet symptomatic. And then, they start having sex. It's the most graphic, gratuitous sex I've ever seen on screen. Midway through, Laura turns into a rabid zombie and rips out "Patrick's" jugular, spraying blood everywhere. And just like that, "Laura" spends the rest of the movie wandering around, completely nude, covered in blood.

Laura let out a disdainful sigh next to me. *Jesus,* she muttered under her breath.

Danielle Simmons, who played her, didn't seem to mind stripping down for the role. She even mentioned in interviews that it was "no big deal." But watching that on the big screen completely violated who Laura was.

As much as I hated what I saw, part of me still wanted to give Patrick the benefit of the doubt. Maybe he didn't fully understand what he was doing. Perhaps he got carried away. Maybe... he'd just gotten too far lost in his own desire to make something "provocative." I tried to think back to when I first met him, how he had seemed enthusiastic about telling real stories. Maybe this was just a misguided effort.

But every scene that followed felt worse than the last.

Victoria Bell, who played my mother, looked eerily like Susan. The brown wig and makeup transformed her, and for a second, I felt a pang of something like admiration for how closely they captured my mom's look. But that vanished the moment she opened her mouth. Every time "Susan" appeared on screen, I held my breath, bracing for the worst.

Early in the movie, "Susan" was a competent doctor who explained rabies and the symptoms of infection. I kept praying they wouldn't disrespect her character, but they reduced her to a caricature as the film wore on.

I started questioning myself, wondering if I was being too sensitive. Maybe the film wasn't *that* bad, and my personal attachment to Susan and Alex was clouding my judgment. But then again, how could it not? They were my family. And Patrick had taken them—all of us—and twisted our memories into something grotesque.

And then, there was Alex.

They cast six-year-old Sammy Evans, a soap opera regular, to play Alex. It was weird watching him as a little kid when my brother had been in his late teens. It wasn't a bad casting choice—just strange. "Alex" acted as the peacemaker between "Ethan" and "Susan," as if he were the only adult in the room. Watching that dynamic was jarring because it reminded me of how mature Alex had been for his age—always calm and rational. The movie tried to mimic that, but it felt forced and unnatural.

I gripped the armrest, trying to convince myself that I could make it through to the end. I thought about confronting Patrick afterward—maybe there was a way to salvage something from this disaster. Maybe I could offer him my perspective and help him see the damage he had done. But with every passing minute, it felt more and more hopeless.

Liam Martinez, who played Craig, was the only one of us not butchered by the script. "Craig" was portrayed as a good guy, friendly with everyone. There was even a subplot where "Craig" considered quitting acting to study journalism, an idea shoehorned in as a tribute to Patrick's need to give every character a more profound "arc."

But the worst came in the third act when Patrick crossed a line I'll never forgive.

"Susan" gets attacked by zombies. They claw at her like animals, tearing her clothes off. Her screams were raw and visceral—like something out of a nightmare. They rip at her flesh while she screams in agony. The scene was grotesque. When she finally succumbs to the infection, she joins the ranks of the infected, stumbling around naked like "Laura" but without the blood—just covered in bruises and gashes.

I sat there, my hands clenched in my lap, remembering my mom, who had spent her life helping people who deserved better than this humiliating, horrific portrayal.

Then came Alex's death.

Toward the end, "Ethan" and "Craig" are trying to help "Alex" climb onto a rooftop when "Susan" appears from nowhere, grabs him, and pulls him down. In the next scene, we see "Alex" again, only this time he's infected, crawling toward them on the ground. White foam oozes from his mouth, and he gnashes his teeth together like a rabid animal. His right leg has been torn off.

As "Alex" crawled, I flashed back to a Christmas years ago, when Alex flew to L.A. to spend the holidays with me. I remembered his laugh, his shy smile, the way he'd always try to keep the peace. And now I was watching this grotesque version of him, crawling and screeching like a monster.

The final blow came when a military truck appeared out of nowhere and ran over "Alex." Blood and entrails left a trail on the street, smeared across the pavement.

That's when Laura and I stood up and left the theater.

We didn't speak. We didn't stop for reporters or fans outside. Usually, I'd at least acknowledge them out of courtesy, but not that night. I was too angry—afraid I'd say something I couldn't take back.

Of course, *The Plague* was a hit. Critics called it the best zombie movie in years. The rave reviews made my blood boil. I took sick satisfaction in the rare bad reviews, where people called it exploitative and violent, accusing Patrick of sensationalizing actual events. It was petty, but every bad review felt like justice.

Even then, though, part of me wondered if I was overreacting. Maybe the movie wasn't as bad as I thought—maybe it was my grief talking. But deep down,

I knew that wasn't the case. I knew the film had crossed a line, and I couldn't ignore that.

Kevin hounded me for interviews, but I refused every single one. Craig hadn't even seen the movie, and he made it clear he had no interest.

Then, one day, a reporter who hadn't seen *The Plague* herself reached out for my thoughts. Kevin pushed me to do it, and after months of dodging, I finally agreed.

"Calling *The Plague* trash is an insult to trash," I told her. It summed up the interview. But she couldn't leave it there.

"You seem to have a lot of strong feelings about the movie," she pressed. "Is it because you had no involvement?"

I wanted to leap across the table and wring her smug neck, but I kept my cool. "Patrick asked if I wanted to be involved. I declined."

She scribbled down some notes and then asked the question I knew was coming. "Was it too painful? Because your mother and brother—"

"Yes," I cut her off. "Of course."

The interview was published shortly after, and that's when Patrick called.

"I read the article," he said. "I think we should talk."

"Yeah, I'll be there," I replied.

Talk to the writer and director of *The Plague* about what I thought of his movie? You bet your ass I'd be there.

26

Patrick could tell what kind of meeting it would be when I didn't shake his hand after he extended it to me.

"What the hell were you thinking?" I asked, my voice barely controlled.

He didn't answer with an apology or even an explanation. Instead, he launched into a lecture. "Ethan, a negative review from a newspaper, no matter how reputable, can't hurt ticket sales. But from a celebrity, especially one who practically tells people not to see it? That's different."

"I never told people not to see it," I shot back.

"You might as well have. You called it trash, Ethan. *Trash.*"

I held my tongue, though I wanted to scream that the movie *was* trash. But that wouldn't help the conversation.

"I was being honest. You know the definition of the word 'honest,' right?"

Patrick's eyes narrowed into a glare. "What's that supposed to mean?"

I leaned forward in my chair. "It means your movie was a bullshit exploitation of real people—people who died."

Patrick let out a short laugh as if my words were beneath him. "It's a zombie movie. Shit that could never really happen, Ethan."

"There's a title card at the beginning that says the movie is inspired by a true story," I countered.

"Inspired isn't the same as based, and you know it."

I could feel my frustration rising. "Making me look bad is one thing, Patrick. I'm an actor; I can take it. But disrespecting my mother and brother? Two people who *died* because of that outbreak. God, Patrick, the way you showed my mother—naked, covered in blood..."

He cut me off. "Because that's what sells. Naked tits sell tickets. Blood on naked tits? Even more. I'm sorry about what happened to your mom and brother, but that's the kind of shit people want to watch."

"They want to watch a young child get run over by a fucking truck?" I asked, my voice shaking.

"Yes!" Patrick shot back, leaning forward. "Jesus, Ethan, you're acting like I made a snuff film."

I gripped the arms of my chair so hard that my knuckles turned white. Every instinct told me to leap over that desk and throttle him. The only thing stopping me was the last bit of self-control I had left. "You could've made this movie without tying it to the Ivywood outbreak," I said through clenched teeth.

Patrick shook his head. "Water under the bridge now. It's a work of fiction, Ethan. Don't get so worked up."

I stood up, my control slipping. "Seriously? People are dead, Patrick."

He slammed his fists down on his desk, his face red. "Enough! It's a zombie movie! How many times do I have to say it?"

I felt my own temper flare. "You created a zombie movie that disrespected a real tragedy."

His voice dropped, but the intensity didn't. "Yeah, it was tragic. I'm sorry people got sick. I'm sorry some people had to be hospitalized. And I'm especially sorry some people died, including your mom and brother. But look at all the movies made about World War II. Nobody bitches about those."

I was dumbfounded. "Those are done in a *respectful* manner, Patrick."

He shrugged, leaning back in his chair with a smug smile. "Well, I don't own a time machine. What's done is done. What happened was horrible, but why not make a little money from it? Making money never hurt anyone."

And that did it.

"You're disgusting, and I hope everyone who was affected by that outbreak sues the ever-living shit out of you," I spat, my voice trembling with rage.

Patrick didn't flinch. "Get the hell out of my office. You're done, Ethan. *Done!*"

I slammed the door on my way out. Patrick didn't have the power to blacklist me, but in Hollywood, whispers could spread fast. One director's opinion could make other executives wary. Still, I knew Patrick wasn't big enough to ruin my career, but his arrogance and indifference made me sick.

I stormed out of the building, the warm L.A. air slapping my face as I made my way to the car. My phone buzzed in my pocket. I saw Laura's name on the screen.

"Hey, honey," I answered, trying to keep my voice steady.

"How did it go?" she asked gently. She was on set in New York, filming an independent romantic comedy. I could hear the concern in her voice.

I told her the whole story, my anger bubbling just beneath the surface. "I'm sorry," she said, her tone sympathetic. "It's easier said than done, but try not to let it get to you."

She was right. Laura always knew what to say to keep me grounded. But as I merged onto the freeway, the heat from the broken A/C and the weight of the conversation with Patrick pressed down on me. The traffic felt suffocating, worse than usual, and I couldn't shake the image of my mom and brother from my mind.

By the time I got home, my head was pounding, and all I wanted to do was collapse. An invitation to a stakeholder's party at *The Oracle* was in the mail, courtesy of Luke. A party was exactly what I needed—a chance to see friends and maybe put *The Plague* behind me for a night.

When Laura returned from New York, she joined me at Luke's event. The atmosphere was warm and celebratory, and for the first time in weeks, I felt a sense of peace. Laura looked stunning in her satin dress, the same one she wore to *The Plague* premiere. Before we left for the party, she asked if I wanted her to wear something different, worried the dress might bring back bad memories.

"It's fine," I told her. "You look beautiful."

At the party, Luke's wife, Amanda, and Laura spent the evening catching up while Luke and I stood by the bar. Between sips of gin and tonics, I recounted my confrontation with Patrick. Luke listened intently, throwing in a much-needed "What an asshole" every now and then.

Every time I glanced at Laura across the room, her beauty made me forget about Patrick, the movie, and everything else that had been weighing me down. It was impossible to feel bad with her there, lighting up the room.

At the party, Luke's brother, Adam, received a touching toast. After years of struggling with alcohol abuse and countless rehab stints, Adam finally turned his life around.

Luke announced that Adam would manage the newest Fairchild Hotel in San Diego. The whole room stood to applaud him. Watching Adam wipe away tears of gratitude reminded me of the bond Alex and I had shared—the quiet, unspoken support we had always given each other.

I missed him. I missed them both.

But that night, surrounded by friends and family, I felt a little more hopeful. Maybe I'd find my way through this after all.

27

Word quickly got out that I wasn't a fan of *The Plague*.

There was no doubt Patrick had something to do with it, but he wasn't the only one at fault. Every media outlet seemed to want my opinion, and I wasn't shy about giving it. I told them the truth—*The Plague* was exploitative, sensationalized, and downright disrespectful. When reporters pushed back (especially those who enjoyed the movie), I reminded them that Patrick used real people involved in the outbreak as characters, including my family members who had died.

Some reporters offered polite condolences for my loss. Others weren't so kind. Entertainment reporter Jared Wells went as far as to suggest I was being overly sensitive because, "It's only a movie, and people know that Susan and Alex didn't die so horrifically."

"Go fuck yourself," I snapped, and even though they bleeped the expletive out when it aired, the clip was replayed over and over on TV and online, becoming an infamous sound bite. Jared's face went from smug to mortified, but I didn't care. I stormed out of the studio, leaving behind the chaos of my anger.

That interview—and the ones that followed about *The Plague*—made my career nosedive faster than I could have imagined.

The first sign was the roles. I went from getting steady small parts in TV shows and movies to barely booking anything. My film work dwindled to shorts, and my TV roles shrank to one or two lines. I played roles that an extra with a SAG card could've filled. It wasn't very comfortable, but at least I was still working. I knew actors whose careers had crashed so hard they were waiting tables at random restaurants within months of being on a hit show.

I clung to that thought: *At least I'm still working*.

By early 2015, I landed the lead in a theatrical production called *Breaking the Silence*. The play was about a man who goes to therapy for PTSD caused by traumatic childhood events and eventually forms a complicated romantic relationship with his psychiatrist. It was a meaty role, and the execution was phenomenal—thanks to the talented playwright, Donald Westbrook. We performers had a lot to work with, and the reviews reflected it. One critic wrote, "Ethan Mitchell returns in fine form," while another claimed, "If you're an aspiring actor, Mitchell's performance exemplifies what great acting is."

That kind of praise made me feel like I was back on track and hadn't lost my touch. It was the first time in years I felt genuinely proud of my work. But just when I thought things were looking up, Kevin called me out of the blue.

"I'm sorry, Ethan, but I've got to drop you as a client. You're not bringing in the money anymore, and I need to focus on my other clients," he said.

Hearing those words from Kevin hit me like a punch to the gut. He had been my agent for years, guiding my career from its early days when I transitioned from modeling to acting. He was the one who believed in me when no one else did. Connor had introduced us, and we'd been a team ever since. Hearing him say I wasn't worth his time anymore felt like a betrayal.

"I'm doing *Breaking the Silence*," I reminded him, my voice tight with desperation. I didn't want to beg, but I also didn't want to be discarded like yesterday's news.

"Yeah, but it's theater, man. It's not bringing in the big bucks," Kevin said, his voice lacking any trace of the warmth we once shared.

And just like that, it was over.

I hung up, feeling numb. Laura tried to comfort me later that night, rubbing my back and offering words of solace. She explained how Hollywood worked, how it could be cutthroat and cruel. "They treat you like royalty as long as you're making them money," she said. "But the second you stop, you're just another nobody."

Her words were true, but they didn't make it any easier. I knew how Hollywood worked. I'd been in the game long enough to know the rules. But that didn't make the sting of rejection any less painful. Kevin had been more than just an agent—he was a partner, someone who had helped me climb the ladder of success. And now, I was just another client he didn't need.

I tried to keep going. I went to open auditions, hoping to land a role on my own. But nothing came of it. No callbacks, no smiles from casting agents. I wasn't even worth a second glance. Hunting for new representation was no better. Most agents didn't bother returning my calls, and those who did politely told me they weren't seeking new clients.

For a moment, I wondered if Patrick had blacklisted me. Or maybe I'd done it to myself by criticizing his movie in such a public way. The entertainment reporters, with their twisted words, had certainly played their part, painting me as some spoiled Hollywood brat who couldn't handle criticism.

But deep down, I knew the truth. I wasn't a bankable star anymore. Why would an agent or manager represent me if I couldn't book even the smallest role? No roles meant no money—for me or them. Hollywood didn't care about the past. It only cared about what you could bring to the table right now.

It was a hard pill to swallow, but I had to admit it: Hollywood was done with me.

I thought back to how I'd gotten my start with Kevin. Desperate, I tried to remember the exact moment he signed me. I vaguely recalled performing a monologue that impressed him, but the details were fuzzy. So much had happened since then.

For a brief moment, I considered going back to modeling. But when I looked in the mirror one morning, fresh out of the shower, I saw a body that was no longer chiseled like a Greek god. The six-pack was nearly a keg. Sure, I wasn't in terrible shape—I didn't have a dad bod—but I certainly wasn't going to book any modeling gigs either.

It was hard to accept, but the reality stared me in the face every time I looked in the mirror. Hollywood had moved on, and I was the only one who hadn't. I needed to let go. I needed to move on, too.

But admitting that my career in Hollywood was over? That was the hardest thing I've ever done.

28

Breaking the Silence ended its run in December 2016.

The night of our last show was memorable, but not just because we closed a successful run. It marked something more significant—the official end of my acting career.

Laura had pleaded with me not to give up. "You have such immense talent," she said, her voice hopeful. She even dreamed of us working together again on another project. "Remember how fun it was on *Country Doctors*? Imagine doing a movie or another show together," she would say, trying to reignite my passion.

And it was fun—working alongside her had been one of the highlights of my career. But that part of my life felt like a closed chapter, one I couldn't go back to. As much as I loved acting, I had to face reality.

"Remember when you first moved out here, how hard it was to get started?" Laura reminded me one night. I gave her a small nod. "Reigniting your career should be easier now because, unlike before, people know who you are."

I reminded her that none of it mattered. "Not a single agent or manager wants to meet with me anymore. I haven't booked a single role in months, even after all those casting calls."

She looked at me with sad eyes, the kind that told me she was heartbroken for me but didn't know how to help. *It's a sign,* I thought to myself as I said aloud, "My acting career is over, and it's something I have to accept."

Those were the hardest words I'd ever said. What was even harder was realizing that I was unemployed for the first time in my adult life. Laura was now the breadwinner, and while Luke and I were business partners, I wasn't earning much. I was a silent partner, which meant I was more of an investor than anything else.

As much as I tried to bury the thought, I couldn't stop it from creeping into my mind: *What if acting had been my only shot? What if there was nothing left for me?*

One afternoon, Luke and I met for lunch at a small café just off Rodeo Drive. It was a chance to catch up. He asked me how things were going, and I told him the truth—that my acting career was over and I didn't know what to do next. Like so many others in the industry, I had nothing to fall back on. My entire life had been wrapped up in acting, and now, that was gone.

Luke, as always, was supportive. He didn't rush to give advice; he listened, letting me vent my frustrations. That's one of the reasons we've always gotten along—Luke has a way of making you feel heard.

After a long pause, Luke suddenly asked, "Did you ever consider teaching?"

I stared at him, mid-bite of my chicken tenders, not sure if I'd heard him right. He leaned forward, his eyes locked on mine, waiting for an answer. I thought about stalling, maybe asking him to clarify what he meant, but I knew exactly what he was asking.

"I've never thought about it," I admitted with a shrug.

"You'd make a good teacher," Luke said, his tone confident.

I took a drink of my water. "I don't have any experience. Don't schools require teachers to have the proper credentials or accreditation?"

Luke shrugged. "Maybe, but it's not like you're trying to teach high school math. You've got years of experience in the industry. I'm sure you've got something to offer students." Then he hit me with a question that shook me to my core: "What else do you have to fall back on that isn't acting-related?"

Damn. I hated how right he was. What the hell did I have to fall back on? Modeling was out of the question—I no longer have the build for it. Washing dishes or bussing tables again? I wouldn't be able to pay for a month's worth of bills with a year's worth of wages from that job, not with the house and the lifestyle Laura and I had. The thought of it was both humbling and terrifying.

"Nothing, I guess," I finally said.

"Then go for it! What do you have to lose?"

"I wouldn't know where to start," I said, feeling a little lost.

"There's that private university up in Pasadena," Luke suggested. "I think it's called Sunny Hills. Why not check it out?"

I knew the school—*Sunny Hills Conservatory*. I'd heard about it in passing but never thought of it as a potential workplace. One of Luke's part-time employees was a student there, which was probably why he thought of it. I nodded, letting the idea settle in. It was so foreign to me, this notion of teaching. But the more I thought about it, the more it made sense.

Acting had been my life for over a decade. But maybe now, I could transition to teaching the next generation of actors. I had the experience, the stories, and the lessons learned from my successes and failures. It wasn't the dream I'd once had, but it could be a new chapter, something worth exploring.

Still, doubt gnawed at me. Would students even take me seriously? I wasn't an academic—I was an actor who had stumbled into teaching as a backup plan. Would they see through me? Would I see through myself?

"So... does that sound like something you might be interested in?" Luke asked, snapping me out of my thoughts.

I smiled, but it felt more like a mask. "It's definitely something to think about."

After lunch, I drove to Sunny Hills Conservatory to inquire about teaching positions. It might have been unorthodox to show up without an appointment, but as an actor, I was used to walking into auditions and meetings with little notice. This was no different, I told myself.

When I arrived, I parked and walked across the campus. The parking lot was packed, and students were everywhere. With each step, the nervousness in my stomach grew. By the time I reached the administration building, my stomach felt like it was tied in knots.

As I reached for the door handle, I heard a girl's voice behind me. "Oh my God, it's Ethan Mitchell!"

I turned to find a young woman running toward me, her long blonde hair blowing in the breeze and a stack of textbooks clutched to her chest. Her name was Molly, and she couldn't have been older than twenty-one.

"Ethan, I'm such a big fan! Can I get a picture?" she asked, her eyes wide with excitement.

"Of course," I said, forcing a smile despite the anxiousness swirling inside me. It had been a while since someone had asked for a picture, and I felt a strange mix of nostalgia and unease.

Molly snapped a quick selfie with me before asking, "What are you doing here? Are you giving a guest lecture or something?"

For a moment, I hesitated. What would she think if I told her I was looking for a job? Would she still see me as the actor she admired?

"I'm thinking about teaching," I finally said.

Her face lit up with the biggest smile I'd ever seen. "That is so cool! If you do, I'm totally taking your class!"

"Thank you," I said, returning her smile. Her enthusiasm was reassuring, and I silently thanked her for making me feel like maybe this new path wasn't so crazy after all.

As I watched Molly hurry off to class, I realized that being recognized by fans might become a rare occurrence. That part of my life was slowly fading, and I had to accept it.

When I reached the entrance to the administration building, I paused again. My heart was racing. I had faced some of the toughest challenges in Hollywood, yet here I was, feeling nervous about opening a door. I took a deep breath, told myself to calm down, and finally pulled it open.

It was time to see what the future held.

29

Surprisingly, Dr. Joyce Sinclair, who was – and still is – the head of the Department of Performing Arts at Sunny Hills Conservatory, watched as I nervously stumbled into the lobby.

"You're Ethan Mitchell," she greeted, her voice warm but steady. The receptionist she had been talking to stared at me, her mouth hanging open.

"I certainly am!" I smiled, trying to hide the nervousness bubbling up inside me.

Dr. Sinclair strolled up to me. My first impression of her was that she was confident, polite, and professional. She extended her hand, and I shook it firmly. "How may I help you? Are you considering taking a course or two?" she asked, her smile suggesting she was teasing just a little.

"If I'm being honest, I was wondering if there are any teaching positions available?" Right after asking, I cringed internally. This wasn't like waltzing into a fast-food joint and asking for an opening. Teaching felt like an entirely different universe.

Dr. Sinclair thought for a moment, and then her smile widened. "Let's discuss this in my office."

Once we took our seats in her office, she broke the news to me that no full-time teaching positions were available. However, she quickly added, "How would you feel about being a guest lecturer? You could talk to our students about your career—how you got started, what it takes to maintain a career, and share some insights about the realities of the industry."

Guest lecturing hadn't even crossed my mind, but the idea was intriguing. It wasn't a full commitment but could help me test the waters.

"I'd be happy to," I said, standing up with a smile, extending my hand this time.

Dr. Sinclair—Joyce—took it enthusiastically. "That's wonderful, Mr. Mitchell. Thank you so much." She then went over the logistics—a date and time were set, and she mentioned they would offer me an honorarium. Though the pay wasn't Hollywood-level, I didn't care. Honestly, I would've done it for free.

When I got home and told Laura the news, she lit up. "You'll be great," she said, immediately offering to help me prepare. We spent the next few days with her playing the role of a curious acting student, throwing in random questions to make sure I could think on my feet. Laura's insights were invaluable, especially when she suggested which stories to include and which ones to leave out—like the whole ordeal with Tina Jensen and her stalker. Some memories were better left untouched.

The process of writing the lecture brought back waves of nostalgia. It was funny how quickly my early career in Hollywood had become something I looked back on, like a distant memory. Those early days—the struggle, the excitement of booking my first gig, and even the awkward modeling jobs—now felt like a lifetime ago.

Once the lecture was ready, I practiced it in front of Laura a few times. She was my harshest critic, but she knew exactly how to help me tweak the delivery. "You need to emphasize this part more," she would say, or, "You might want to slow down here. Let it breathe."

I was more nervous than I expected on the day of the lecture. It wasn't stage fright—I had performed in front of cameras and live audiences for years—but this was different. This was me, not a character, standing in front of students eager to learn from my real-life experiences.

The auditorium was packed. Dr. Sinclair introduced me with a warm and flattering speech, and as I stepped up to the podium, the applause was deafening. It felt surreal. I glanced toward the audience and spotted Laura smiling encouragingly. Seeing her and Joyce in the front row helped steady me.

I took a deep breath and started my lecture. My voice trembled at first, but as I got into the flow of telling my story—the highs and lows of my career—I felt more comfortable. The students were engaged, leaning forward in their seats, some scribbling notes as I spoke about my first audition, how I had bombed it, and what I learned from the experience. Their enthusiasm fed my energy.

Midway through, I shared one of the more personal moments from my career—how I almost gave up acting after being rejected by nearly every casting director in town. I wanted them to understand that success isn't linear, that it's a rollercoaster of triumphs and setbacks.

Then came the Q&A. Most of the questions were predictable but thoughtful: "How did you prepare for your roles?" "What's the hardest part of being in the industry?" I answered each with the honesty and openness I had promised myself I'd bring to this lecture.

Then Molly, the student I had met on campus, raised her hand. "How do you handle the pressure of public scrutiny and media attention?" she asked.

It was a great question, and it caught me a little off-guard. "It can be challenging," I admitted. "But it's important to stay focused on why you got into this business in the first place—your love for the craft. There will always be opinions about you, and not all of them will be kind.

That's where having a strong support system helps. For me, that's been my friends and my amazing wife, Laura."

I glanced at Laura, who beamed at me from the audience. For a moment, I forgot about the students and the lecture. All I saw was her—my rock through it all.

As I answered Molly's question, old memories from Hollywood came flooding back—the tabloid stories, the harsh criticism, the betrayal of *The Plague*. I could feel that familiar bitterness rising inside me, but I forced it down. This wasn't the time for that. Instead, I smiled, trying to keep the mood light.

After the Q&A ended, the room erupted in applause again. To my surprise, the students stood up, giving me a standing ovation. Laura was on her feet, too, pride shining in her eyes. I felt a surge of emotion I hadn't felt in a long time—gratitude—for the students, Laura, and even Joyce, who made this opportunity possible.

As soon as the applause died down, Joyce hurried over, shaking my hand excitedly. "That was fantastic, Ethan! Are you sure this was your first time giving a lecture?"

I laughed. "Yes, it was!"

"Well, you could've fooled me," she said, still smiling. "Please, call me Joyce from now on."

We spent the next half-hour mingling with the students, signing autographs, and taking pictures. So many of them told me how much they missed *Country Doctors* and how much the show had meant to them. It was humbling. I missed the show, too, but mostly, I missed the experience of working on it.

I felt a strange sense of calm as Laura and I walked out of the lecture hall into the cool evening air. The bitterness I'd felt toward Hollywood hadn't disappeared entirely, but it had dulled. The lecture had given me something new to focus on—a potential future outside of acting, one where I could still contribute to the craft in a meaningful way.

"I'm so proud of you," Laura said, squeezing my hand.

I stopped and turned to face her, gently touching her shoulders. "I love you," I said softly, and we kissed. It was a brief moment of intimacy before we heard footsteps approaching—students leaving the lecture hall. We broke apart, laughing.

"Well, we'll continue that at home," I said with a grin, and Laura laughed, her hand still in mine as we made our way back to the car.

30

2018 went down as one of the best years of my life.

The highlight, without a doubt, was the birth of our daughter, Jane. New parents often describe the overwhelming joy and excitement that comes with seeing their child for the first time, but until that day in July, I thought it was all a bunch of mushy BS.

I couldn't have been more wrong.

When Laura first announced that she was pregnant, my emotions were all over the place—intense nervousness, fear, and an unshakable feeling that I wasn't ready to be a parent.

I kept thinking, *What the hell do I know about raising a child?* Babysitting Alex for a few hours or even a full day was one thing, but parenting was forever.

And yet, the moment I laid eyes on Jane, all those fears evaporated. There she was, this tiny little person, and suddenly nothing else mattered. The love and joy that filled me were unlike anything I'd ever experienced. For hours after her birth, I couldn't stop smiling, even through the tears. I thought hugging Laura after my first guest lecture was euphoric, but that feeling didn't even come close.

The other major milestone came several months later, in December. I got a call from Dr. Sinclair—Joyce—letting me know that there was an opening for a full-time adjunct professor position at Sunny Hills. She told me before it was even posted on their website, giving me a bit of a head start.

I couldn't believe my luck. But as it turns out, I wasn't *that* lucky. I still had to go through the formal interview process alongside the other candidates. Joyce explained that it was university policy, and while I was confident, it didn't stop the nerves from creeping in.

The interview itself was nerve-wracking, but I pushed through, knowing how much this opportunity meant to me. The members of the hiring committee, many of whom had seen my work in film and television, seemed more interested in my stories from Hollywood than the specifics of my teaching qualifications. But I knew they'd still look closely at how I handled a classroom.

When Joyce finally called to offer me the position, I felt like I had truly found my new path. Teaching felt right in a way that acting hadn't in a long time. After accepting the job, I immediately called Luke and invited him out for a drink at the same bar where we'd first met.

"Congratulations, *Professor* Mitchell," Luke said with a hearty laugh, giving me a few playful slaps on the back. Yes, it was a little cringy, but in his defense, he was on his third beer, and it was a Friday night.

Professor Ethan Mitchell. It had a nice ring to it. As I sipped my drink, I found myself smiling at the thought that my name had gone from being on movie posters to being printed in course catalogs. It was a stretch, but the juxtaposition amused me.

To celebrate the new job, Laura cooked my favorite meal—mostaccioli with meatballs and mushroom sauce, with a side of garlic knots. Jane celebrated with us, too, in her own way, by messily enjoying some spaghetti and meatballs in the form of baby food. Her smile was infectious, and as we sat together, I realized how happy I was with this new chapter of my life.

But later that night, an old thought crept back into my mind as we cleaned up after dinner. *What would Susan and Alex think of my career change?* Alex would have been supportive. I was sure of that. But Susan? I wasn't as confident. Maybe she would have warmed up to the idea, but it still gnawed at me. I didn't dwell on it for too long, though. You can drive yourself crazy thinking about what might have been.

Then there was Jeff.

I emailed him about Jane's birth, even sending a picture of her, and told him about my new teaching position.

His reply was exactly what I expected—bittersweet. He wrote:

"Thank you for sending the picture of Jane. What a cutie! She has your mother's eyes. But don't think this will repair our relationship. All those sleepless nights your mother and I suffered through wasn't fair. Maybe I should let it go, but I can't. If that makes me petty and overly sensitive, so be it. And I noticed your acting career is dead. I'd say, 'I told you so,' but I feel that would be going too far, though I do feel a little vindicated."

Verbatim.

When Laura read his email, she shook her head. "I'm sorry, Ethan, but your dad's cheese is starting to slip off the cracker," she said, making me laugh despite myself. Her ability to lighten even the heaviest moments was one of the many reasons I loved her.

Luckily, I was able to shrug off Jeff's scathing words. I had no time to focus on his continued resentment. I had bigger things to worry about, like preparing for my first day of class. Joyce had asked me to teach *Introduction to Acting*. She explained that the university's policy was for new professors to start with beginner-level courses before moving on to more advanced ones.

On the morning of my first class, I was a wreck. The nerves hit me hard, twisting my stomach in knots. It wasn't just about the teaching—I hadn't been apart from Jane for more than a few hours since she was born. That, combined with the pressure of my new role, made me feel like I was back on my first day in Hollywood.

When I stepped into the classroom, I was met with a full house—every chair was taken, and some students were standing in the back. It was both overwhelming and exhilarating. I took a deep breath and began the class. To my relief, the nerves faded quickly, and I found my rhythm. The students were attentive, and though a few gave me that star-struck look, no one screamed or asked for an autograph.

That was a welcome surprise.

It was the first time in years that I didn't feel like a celebrity but just a regular person doing his job. It felt… right. After class, a few students approached me—not for selfies or signatures but to ask genuine questions about acting. One student even said, "I'm here because I want to learn from someone with real experience, not just theory."

Hearing that was more rewarding than any fan request. Teaching wasn't just about passing on my knowledge. It was about helping the next generation of actors navigate an industry I knew all too well.

At the end of the day, as I drove home to Laura and Jane, I knew I had made the right decision. Teaching gave me a sense of fulfillment I hadn't felt in a long time. No more twelve-hour days on set. No more media scrutiny. I could be home with my family every night, and for the first time, I felt truly at peace with where my life was headed.

Laura's acting career had also slowed down since Jane was born. She wasn't booking as many roles, and while it had been a tough adjustment for her, we both knew it was the right decision for our family. We traded our Malibu mansion for a modest home—no sauna, no hot tub, no floor-to-ceiling windows, and no view of the ocean. But it was ours, and it was perfect for us.

I loved every inch of that house because my two greatest loves, Laura and Jane, were within its walls.

And that was more than enough.

31

February 2020 marked the beginning of my transition into a full-time professor at Sunny Hills Conservatory.

A month later, the COVID-19 pandemic hit.

Even as the virus swept across the world, I didn't let it stop me from teaching. Like most of my colleagues, I quickly transitioned to online classes, and it was a strange adjustment.

Just when I was starting to get the hang of it, I came down with COVID myself, about a month after Governor Gavin Newsom issued the stay-at-home order. It was one of the worst illnesses I'd ever experienced—up there with my bout of E. coli in Ivywood. Thankfully, Laura and Jane didn't catch it, which I consider a small miracle.

I spent two weeks in bed, feeling like I'd been hit by a freight train. It was as if the virus had drained all the energy from my body, leaving me with nothing but exhaustion and fever. I vividly remember lying there, thinking how lucky I was to have Laura take care of me and keep Jane safe. When I finally started to recover, it was a slow process. Even after the fever and fatigue passed, I lost my sense of taste and smell, which didn't return for another four or five months. That part was rough, but at least I no longer felt like death was creeping up on me.

Around the time I was starting to feel like myself again, I got a call from Mike Lewis, the host of the popular podcast *Reel Talk*. He invited me to be a guest on the show to discuss *The Plague* and how Hollywood treated me afterward.

Initially, I declined—still too tired and not wanting to rehash old wounds. But something about getting my side of the story out there changed my mind. After all, I'd spent years trying to move past *The Plague*, and maybe this was my chance to put it to rest once and for all.

Mike scheduled the episode a week later, giving me time to regain some strength. When the day came, I was a little nervous—it was my first podcast experience. But Mike was an engaging host, and the conversation flowed easily.

MIKE: Lots of people already know how you got into acting and that you studied medicine before quitting and moving out here. If you knew then what you know now, would you have stayed on that path and pursued a career in the medical field?

ETHAN: I think about that sometimes, but then I remind myself that if I'd stayed in Minnesota, I never would have met my wife, Laura.

MIKE: Is it hard to imagine life without Laura Preston?

ETHAN: Very. And, of course, that also means I wouldn't have Jane.

MIKE: Let's talk about Jane for a second. If she wanted to become an actress, would you support her, given your disillusionment with Hollywood?

ETHAN: I'd definitely support her, but I'd make sure she knew what she was getting into. I'd tell her that Hollywood can be incredibly cruel and corrupt. I've seen it firsthand, and I wouldn't want her to walk into that world without knowing the risks.

MIKE: Do you think that disillusionment stems from your experiences with *The Plague* and how your family was portrayed?

ETHAN: Absolutely. When I first moved to L.A., I needed my family's support more than ever. It was terrifying to pursue something as uncertain as an acting career. Thank God Alex was there for me.

MIKE: Didn't you once say your mother eventually came around?

ETHAN: She did, yeah.

MIKE: Let's dive into *The Plague*, then. I know it's a touchy subject, but it seems like a perfect example of how Hollywood can be heartless.

ETHAN: That's an understatement. What Patrick did to my family, to my mother and brother, was beyond cruel. It was downright disrespectful. Turning a real tragedy into a gore-filled spectacle for shock value... It still makes me angry.

MIKE: I was pissed off, too, especially after seeing how the movie treated real people. Do you know if Patrick ever faced any legal repercussions?

ETHAN: I think there were a few lawsuits eventually, but I'm not sure. He deserved it, though.

MIKE: I'm surprised you didn't sue him yourself.

ETHAN: Trust me, I thought about it. But in the end, I didn't want to be tied up in a lawsuit. I wanted it to be over.

MIKE: That makes sense. So, was *The Plague* the turning point in your disillusionment with Hollywood?

ETHAN: Surprisingly, no. It wasn't just the movie—it was how people reacted to my opinion of it. I never thought disliking a film could hurt my career as much as it did.

MIKE: Some people said you were "biting the hand that fed you" by criticizing Patrick, the guy who helped launch your career. What's your response to that?

ETHAN: Maybe I was, but I felt justified. The hand that fed me was also feeding me poison. How was I supposed to react when my family was disrespected like that? I had every right to speak out.

MIKE: You make a good point. It's clear that teaching at Sunny Hills has been a positive change for you. Do you think you'll ever return to acting?

ETHAN: No. I'm happy with where I am now. I've moved on.

MIKE: Even if a great script came along?

ETHAN: Even then. I've found something more fulfilling in teaching, and I'm not interested in juggling two careers.

The rest of the podcast was mostly banter, but it was an eye-opener for me. That conversation helped solidify something I had already been feeling—Hollywood didn't need me, and I didn't need Hollywood. It was liberating.

Of course, I'm sure Patrick and others in the industry were furious when they heard it. I wouldn't be surprised if they wanted to wring my neck. But I had my supporters—Laura, Luke, and even Craig, who reached out after hearing the episode. He invited Laura and me to dinner, and that call was a pleasant surprise.

At the time, Craig was dating Toni Thomas, a supermodel from New York. They'd been together for almost a year and seemed smitten. I'd never seen Craig so happy, which was great to see.

We met them at an upscale French restaurant in downtown L.A. When we arrived, I noticed Craig seemed unusually nervous. It wasn't until after we were seated that I found out why.

Midway through dinner, Craig stood up, reached into his jacket pocket, and pulled out a small black ring box. Dropping to one knee in front of Toni, he opened it to reveal a gold ring with a stunning diamond.

"Toni Thomas, will you marry me?" he asked, his voice shaky but full of love.

Toni's hands flew to her mouth in surprise, and after a moment of shock, she jumped to her feet and shouted, "Yes!" The entire restaurant applauded, with a few people even giving them a standing ovation. It was a beautiful moment, and as I watched Craig slide the ring onto Toni's finger, I couldn't help but reflect on how much he'd changed since we first met.

After dinner, Craig pulled me aside and asked if I would be his best man. It was an honor I gladly accepted. I never would have imagined back in 2007 that Craig and I would become such close friends, let alone that he'd ask me to stand by his side on his wedding day.

Life has a way of surprising you. People change, careers change, and sometimes change for the better.

Craig's growth and my new career as a professor were proof of that.

Final Thoughts

Laura recently did a TV movie where she played a museum employee who finds an ancient artifact that grants her five wishes, all of which backfire in horrible—yet TV-friendly—ways.

We watched it the other day, much to Laura's chagrin (the movie sucked, and she insisted I include that here). While we sat there, half-laughing at the absurdity of it, I started thinking about what I would wish for if such an object really existed.

This is assuming, of course, that the wishes wouldn't backfire.

First, I'd wish to mend my relationship with Jeff. We still haven't patched things up, and at this point, I'm not sure it'll ever happen. Part of me clings to hope, though, mostly because I want Jane and Sue—who was born in 2022—to know their grandfather. It's strange to think about how much time has passed since our last real conversation. When I look at my daughters, I wonder if Jeff even thinks about them or if his bitterness toward me has swallowed up any potential connection with them.

I sometimes imagine going back to specific moments with Jeff, times when I could have said something different, acted with more understanding, or at least tried harder to bridge the gap. I wonder if those little shifts could have changed the trajectory of our relationship.

But then again, some things are just beyond fixing. Maybe that's something I need to accept.

Speaking of Jane and Sue, my second wish is to help them follow their own paths, uninfluenced by Laura or me. While I wouldn't oppose them going into acting, it's a profession that demands total commitment. Acting, especially in Hollywood, is cutthroat. If you're not fully prepared, it can chew you up and spit you out.

I've seen it happen. I've lived it.

California's not cheap, and I don't want my daughters to face the kind of financial uncertainty I did early on, scraping by with low-paying jobs while chasing a dream that may or may not come true.

Maybe it's just the protective father in me, but I don't want them to go through that unless they're 100% sure it's what they want. Acting is a beautiful, rewarding career but also full of hidden pitfalls. I was fortunate to avoid some of the worst of it, but that doesn't mean Jane or Sue would have the same luck.

My third wish would be for Laura and me to continue finding peace and happiness. Hollywood doesn't always deliver that, despite the glamorous facade. Sure, there were perks: luxury cars, a mansion in Malibu, designer clothes. But those things don't bring true peace.

I think about some of the more surreal experiences I've had, like filming that scene in *The Craze* with the tiger. There is nothing peaceful about staring down one of the world's most dangerous predators. Those moments felt larger than life but didn't make me happy.

What *does* bring me happiness is the life Laura and I have built together. We've been through a lot, both in our careers and our personal lives, yet here we are—grounded, laughing together, navigating the ups and downs. We're not perfect, but we've managed to find balance, and that's something I wish for us to keep for the rest of our lives.

My fourth wish would be to come to terms with the fact that some things can't be fixed. This ties back to my first wish about Jeff but also to Susan and Alex.

No, I can't bring them back, and I know that. Still, a part of me wrestles with the thought that if I hadn't pursued acting, we wouldn't have been in Ivywood during the outbreak. They wouldn't have gotten sick, and maybe—just maybe—they'd still be alive.

Logically, I know it's a pointless thought, like swatting at mosquitos at a barbecue. You can try to dodge them, but they'll still find you. As much as I tell myself to let go of that guilt, it comes back, haunting me in quiet moments. Maybe one day, I'll be able to accept it fully.

For my fifth and final wish, I'd wish never to stop dreaming. Dreams are what carried me from a kid in Minnesota with vague aspirations to an actor in Hollywood, living a life I never thought possible.

I wouldn't have made it as an actor if I had stopped dreaming.

I wouldn't have met Laura or had Jane and Sue.

I wouldn't have found my second career as an acting professor, which has brought me more fulfillment than I ever expected.

If I could only have one wish, I'd choose this one. Because even with all the other unresolved parts of my life—the things I can't change or fix—my dreams have always been the driving force that kept me moving forward. Without them, none of this would have been possible.

Dreams don't just guide us; they shape us. I've encouraged every one of my students to follow their dreams, no matter how hard it gets. Because the journey, not the destination, is where the magic happens.

As I sit here typing, I glance over at Sue, chewing on the ear of her teddy bear—something Alex used to do when he was her age. It makes me smile, and sometimes I call her "my little Alex" because she reminds me so much of him. I even considered naming her Alexandra, but that felt like too much. Still, she carries his spirit in little ways, and that brings me comfort.

Before I start rambling (which I do often, thanks to my lecturing), let me offer a few pieces of advice.

First, if you want to become an actor, be prepared for the grind. It's not easy, and it's not quick.

You'll have to work hard, and there will be nights when you wonder if it's worth it. I scrubbed grease from pans and mopped floors while auditioning, and I barely scraped by. I got lucky, but luck alone isn't enough—you've got to put in the effort, too.

Second, burning bridges is something you have to handle with care.

It's rarely a good idea, but sometimes it's necessary—for your career and for your sanity. Just know that once you burn a bridge, it's hard to rebuild it. Choose carefully.

Lastly, and maybe most importantly, live your life.

Yes, pursue your career with everything you've got, but don't forget to live along the way. Take time to step back, breathe, and enjoy the moments with your loved ones. Work is important, but it's not everything. You only get one life—don't waste it.

Thank you for reading this memoir. I hope you found it inspiring, enlightening, and maybe even a little entertaining. If you're one of my fans, thank you for your support through the highs and lows. I'm grateful for each and every one of you.

My acting journey is over, but it was one hell of a ride.

About the Author

Derek Rushlow started writing stories when he was a little boy.

When he grew up, his passion for storytelling remained. It wasn't until 2016 when he not only published his first piece of fiction, but also began working for the YouTube channel, *Planet Dolan*, as a writer/editor. He was with the channel until 2021.

He calls Minnesota home.

X (Twitter): @DerekRushlow

Printed in Great Britain
by Amazon